THE ONE FOR ME

RACHEL HANNA

*T*wenty Years Earlier...

The ocean waves crashed to the shore, and her heart pounded. She'd never kissed a boy before, and certainly not one this good looking. Every girl in school wanted him, and he'd chosen her.

She climbed gingerly up the rock, hoping like heck she didn't slip and look like a fool. Her parents would kill her if they knew where she was right now. They didn't like him. He was too adventurous, too wild, too loud. And his mother was single. She would never understand why that mattered at all, but to her parents that was like a Scarlet letter painted across his chest.

"Are you cold?" he asked. He was always making sure she was okay. He carried her books to class for her. He held her hand when she gave blood at school last week. And yet he hadn't kissed her. Did he even want to?

"No, I'm fine. It's beautiful out here today," she said, trying to hide the anxiety in her voice. Most of her friends had kissed a boy by now. She was almost fifteen years old, after all. Sissy Crawford had kissed three boys already. One was ugly, but she still kissed him trying to improve her odds of finding Mr. Right. Of course, Sissy was no catch herself.

Lucy Williams had kissed Todd Oliver last week, and then she had sex with him. There was no way she was going that far. She wanted to save that for the man she would marry one day. Wasn't that what the honeymoon was for? Her friends thought the idea was nuts, but she thought it was romantic. She wanted to save that "gift" for her husband.

He snuggled up against her and they lay back against the rock, looking up at the cloudless, blue sky. It was early spring, and the ocean breeze was crisp and cool. Not many people were on Emerald Cove Beach today, and that's just the way she wanted it.

"Do you think Mrs. Gill will notice we're gone?" she asked, with a hint of anxiety in her voice.

"Nah. She's so focused on teaching Spanish, she probably won't even realize we're not there."

"Maybe we shouldn't have skipped," she said.

"I couldn't help it," he whispered in her ear. The heat of his breath made her feel tingly all over. "I had to spend some time with you alone. Seeing you in the hall at school isn't cutting it anymore."

She looked over at him and smiled.

"I wanted to be alone with you, too," she said softly. "And my parents won't ever leave us alone when you come to my house."

"I guess that's what parents do," he said. Her parents were going above and beyond in their efforts to "protect" their only daughter and her virtue. Sitting with your mother and father while you watch a movie with your new boyfriend was not her idea of fun.

They sat a few moments longer, and she closed her eyes. Listening to the waves was always calming to her. The seagulls squawked overhead, and maybe that's why she didn't hear him at first.

He leaned in and wrapped his arm around her waist as his mouth came down on hers. The warmth of his lips wrapped around her heart like a warm glove. At first awkward, she joined in the kiss allowing her lips to part and enjoy the moment.

And just then, Jenna Davis knew. She knew that Kyle Parker, popular jock and class clown, would be in her heart forever. She just didn't know how long and winding that journey would end up being for them both.

CHAPTER 1

*K*yle Parker pulled into the driveway of his mother's real estate company and sat in his car, staring at the front of the brick building. For a moment, he was transported back in time, thinking of all those moments when he was a small child running around in the hallways of the large, stately brick office in the square of January Cove.

Living on the coast of Georgia had provided an idyllic childhood in most respects, but it hadn't always been easy for his family. Widowed at thirty-five years old, Adele Parker had raised five kids on her own. Kyle was the second oldest child, just after his brother, Jackson. Not having a father had certainly made him closer to his mother, but it had also penned him in, somewhat.

Feeling like his mother needed him to help her

run the real estate company, Kyle knew that he'd stayed too long already. His dreams weren't housed in the old brick building, full of files and paperwork. His dreams were more about lumber and brick and mortar. As the owner of his new real estate investment company, Kyle had already bought and sold three homes in the last year, renovating each one for a profit.

He knew that it was time to break away from the "family business" and go out on his own. Adele wouldn't be mad at him, quite the opposite, actually. Instead, she would do what she always did and wish him well. She'd always wanted only the best for her kids, and she'd go out of her way to make sure they were happy.

Losing his father when he was only ten years old had been hard on Kyle. When his Dad was killed in a car accident, the whole family changed. His mother had to take over as the sole breadwinner while he and his older brother became fathers to three smaller children.

After working with his mother in the real estate company for the last decade, Kyle had decided it was finally time to venture out on his own. Although he'd started his real estate investment company less than two years ago, he was very successful already. In fact, he was becoming quite well known in January Cove as the person to go to if you were in trouble. People who had suffered through job loss or other economic situations often called on Kyle to buy their house out of foreclosure. He worked with many different kinds of real estate situations from pre-foreclosures to short sales, and he was known as being someone who was fair and honest.

Of course, Kyle would do anything that would make money because he had a huge entrepreneurial spirit. He'd always been the adventurous one of the bunch, but he definitely focused himself when it came to business. Making sure that he never had to suffer again through economic hardship like his mother did when they were children, Kyle always made sure to protect his family and give money to his mom when and if she needed it.

But Adele Parker was not one who would ever ask for a handout. After her husband died, she pulled herself together within the first year and got her real estate license. Building the company from scratch with only a high school education, Adele became well-known in January Cove and the surrounding areas as being one of the best businesswomen around. She'd won awards and mentored other young women, which had always been inspirational to all of her kids.

As Kyle got out of the car and made the short walk into the brick building, he thought about how his mother might react when she found out that he was finally leaving the company for good and striking out on his own. He hoped that she wouldn't be too disappointed in him for leaving the company, but in his heart he knew that she'd be proud of him for doing something on his own.

The three-story brick building had been standing in January Cove since the late 1800s. Adele had gotten a great deal on it when she bought it out of foreclosure, almost twenty-five years ago. Thankfully, their father had a small life insurance policy from his employer when he'd passed away. Because of this, Adele was able to take care of the children without any income for the first year after his death. She was also able to put a small down payment on the building, which she'd finally paid off about ten years after purchasing it.

"Good morning, Kyle," said Jayna, the receptionist at the front desk. She was the perkiest receptionist they'd had at the real estate company in the last few years, and many of the men around town often came into the office just to see her. However, she was quite demure and humble for someone with such great looks. Kyle had made a decision long ago never to date anyone in the office, especially since he was one of the company owners. But, she was fun to look at.

"Good morning, Jayna," Kyle said with a smile. She smiled back, which always let him know that she was interested in him, but he tried not to let it go any further than that after dating one of the former receptionists early on in his career. He quickly learned that feelings and office matters didn't mix very well.

After picking up his mail downstairs, Kyle went up the spiral staircase in the back corner of the building as he usually did. There was another staircase, but Kyle enjoyed going up the old spiral staircase because it was so unique. He loved these kinds of architectural details, which was probably one of the reasons why he got into rehabbing houses in the first place. The idea of turning a fixer-upper house into a real home for a new family was both daunting and exciting at the same time.

As he made his way up to the second floor, he walked to his mother's office, which was on the far end of the building. She'd splurged a few years ago and made her office into exactly what she'd wanted, ornate and gaudy. Adele Parker was quite a character, and her style choices were all her own.

When he walked into Adele's office, he found her sitting behind the desk as she usually was, going over a multitude of contracts. As the head broker, she was at the helm of about twenty agents who worked in January Cove. These agents had been with her for a long time, and they were a force to be reckoned with. Adele was a strong trainer when it came to real estate, and she'd taught all of her agents the right way to market themselves to attract more clients for the company.

"Hey, Mom," Kyle said as he walked behind the

desk and kissed his mother on the cheek. She smiled up at him as usual, with her perky blonde hair and bright blue eyes lit up by the sunlight piercing through the plantation shutters on a nearby window.

"Good morning, son," Adele said. "To what do I owe this pleasure? I thought you were taking the day off."

"Well, I had something I wanted to talk to you about, and I figured it'd be better to go ahead and get it over with now."

"That doesn't sound good," she said with a smile.

"It's not bad news, and I think you know it's coming. Look, Mom, I've had a wonderful time working with you here for the last ten years, but you know that my investment company is taking up more and more of my time…"

"I know exactly what you're talking about, Kyle. You don't have to worry about it. I know that you want to strike out on your own and build your new company. It's okay, son, you don't have to feel guilty about it. I knew this day was coming. And, I'm so proud of you for doing something on your own and building a business. You're going to want that one day when you get married."

"Oh, Mom, I love how you slipped that in there about getting married. You know as well as I do that I'm not the marrying kind."

"Kyle, when you find the right woman one day, you're going to want to get married and have a family of your own. You might not believe it now, mainly because your heart's been broken one too many times, but one of these days you're going to want to have a wife and a family."

Kyle looked at his mom and smiled. He knew better than to argue with her about anything because she'd always find a way to win. She'd spent the last decade trying to marry him off so that she could get one of her kids to produce that first coveted grandchild. She kept complaining that with five grown kids, she should have some grand babies to spoil by now.

But Kyle was convinced that he wouldn't be the one to get married. One major heartbreak in particular, early in his twenties, had caused Kyle to stay away from any kind of committed relationship. Sure, he dated. In fact, he was one of the most eligible bachelors in January Cove. However, he had no interest in settling down with one woman or giving his heart away again. He made that mistake one time, and he wasn't ever going to repeat it.

"Well, I'm glad that you aren't upset at me. I'd never want to do anything to leave you in the lurch, but honestly I don't think you need me anymore. Your business is booming, even in this slow real estate market. When things pick up, you're really going to be looking at a lot of business coming in."

"Honey, I'll always need you. If things don't work out with the investment company, you can always come back. But I hope they work out, for your sake. I know you need to do something that's all your own. Every man needs that in his life."

Leave it to his mother to understand exactly what he needed. She'd always been that way. She was always able to look at each one of her children as individuals and figure out what they needed to succeed in life.

Kyle walked behind the desk as his mother stood up and gave her a hug. Their family had always been close-knit, especially after his father died. While some families might have broken apart in the wake of such tragedy, his family banded together and gotten closer. Each of the five children was very different, but they always had each other's back. And, at the helm, as always, was their mother. She was a fighter and someone they all looked up to.

As Kyle walked back outside to get in his car, he thought about this new beginning. Even though the investment company had already been doing business for a couple of years, this was the final breaking away from his old life. Now, it was all up to him to make sure that he made enough money to support himself and put away for the future. He also needed to make sure that he did enough to help his two employees that he'd just hired in the last six months. This was make-or-break time, and Kyle felt like something fantastic was on the horizon.

Jenna Davis sat on the patio of her quaint home just outside of January Cove, as she did every morning. With a cup of coffee in one hand and a good romance novel in the other, Jenna tried her best to take her mind off of the terrible turn of events her life had taken recently. While her five-year-old daughter, Kaitlyn, was at the local elementary school, Jenna had time to sit and think about what she was going to do next.

Her life had certainly gone in a totally different direction than she'd expected. In high school and early college, she had a boyfriend that meant the world to her. He was everything she'd ever wanted, but her parents didn't approve of him at all. While he was nice and clean-cut, he was quite adventurous and didn't seem to have a firm and direct path for his future. On top of that, he came from a family with a single mother who was always struggling to make ends meet. Her parents didn't feel like that was what Jenna deserved in her life. They wanted her to have someone who had a real career path and would take care of her. They'd allowed her to see him during high school, but when it became important for her future and they thought he was holding her back, they pushed hard to break them up.

Jenna didn't fight with her parents a whole lot, and she was kind of scared of them. It wasn't that her parents were physically or mentally abusive, but they were very direct in what they wanted out of Jenna. She'd always been a straight-A student, and that was mostly because she was afraid of her parents' reaction if she didn't bring home good grades. When she started dating her boyfriend in high school, her mother was none too pleased. She wanted her to focus on her studies and save dating for her college years, which Jenna always thought was crazy but never verbalized to her parents. They were a critical pair, and she always felt like she cowered in the corner when it came to their constant onslaught of opinions.

Of course, now her parents weren't the ones who were in charge of her situation. Her mother had passed away three years ago and her father was in a nursing home with early-onset Alzheimer's. It was probably a good thing that neither of her parents could see where her life ended up because they'd have a lot to say about it. They would blame her no matter what the situation was. Yes, a lot had changed in Jenna's life over the last few years. In fact, the last decade of her life didn't match up at all to where she thought she'd be.

Jenna had always wanted to be an art teacher, yet now she was waiting tables at a rural diner just outside of town. She'd always wanted to have a big family and a happy marriage, yet here she sat, newly divorced in her small home that was about to be foreclosed upon. She was thankful to be a couple of counties over from her hometown of January Cove because the last thing she wanted was to run into her old boyfriend. She imagined a lot of, "I told you so's" would be spewed if she ever saw him again.

Part of the reason for her unhappiness had to be because her parents pushed her into a relationship with a man she never really loved. Forcing her to break up with her high school boyfriend, Jenna was shipped off to college halfway across the country. She'd wanted to major in art, but her parents told her that getting a business degree was the better way to go. She'd done that, but she soon realized that she hated working for any kind of business that didn't involve art in some way. Of course, her mother and father had insisted that art was not a "real" career, and she needed to focus on making money and turning herself into "wife material," as they called it.

While in college, she met Nick, her now ex-husband. He was a premed student planning to go into family medicine, and her mother and father were thrilled that she'd found this man. She didn't really love Nick, but he was nice enough at the time and seemed to have a good career path ahead of him. When she'd come home one summer from college to see her boyfriend, she remembered the painful look in his eyes when she had to explain that she was dating someone else and their five-year relationship was now over. Her heart ached as she drove away, leaving him standing in his driveway with that shell-shocked look on his beautiful face. And the sad part was that she knew it was a mistake, but she just couldn't stand up to her parents.

Jenna had given up most of her dreams long ago. The idea of being an artist when she had a daughter to raise on her own was pushed to the back burner. Instead, she worked her fingers to the bone as a waitress for as many hours as she could get each week, which was never enough. Her ex-husband had fought her tooth and nail about paying alimony and even child support. Dragging her through the court system, he'd used every trick in the book to avoid paying anything even though he caused the divorce with his infidelity in the first place.

She just didn't understand how this man could have a daughter that he rarely saw and then not want to support her financially either. What had she missed in his character and personality that allowed her to make a baby with someone like him?

As with most mornings, Jenna dissolved into tears on her patio, putting her empty coffee cup on the table beside her and throwing her romance novel on the ground. Living life as a single mother with little money was even harder than she'd ever imagined it would be.

CHAPTER 2

*K*yle's morning had started off good, with his mother fully understanding his intentions to build his investment business. Next on his agenda was lunch with his younger brother, Aaron.

Aaron ran another part of Adele's booming real estate business in January Cove — the RV campground. The property was popular all over the Southeast with people coming from miles around to enjoy the quaint beach and fun family activities.

The campground had grown a lot over the years, especially once Aaron took it over three years ago. He stood out as being different in his family with his white blond hair and sparkling blue eyes. He was also the one that everyone thought would be married by now. After dating Natalie Jenkins for three years, there were plans to wed next summer.

Unfortunately, Natalie ended up cheating with a co-worker and breaking Aaron's heart.

Aaron had only been two years old when their father died, and he was the one that Kyle worried most about. He seemed to crave love, even though he'd always had plenty from their mother. He was an outdoorsy guy, always involved in hiking some mountain or rafting down some raging river. He loved to be outside, which was why the campground was such a godsend for him. It kept him gainfully employed after he quit college, and it allowed him to enjoy the great outdoors.

But, still, Kyle worried about his baby brother. He'd been pretty angry since his breakup with Natalie just three months ago. He'd developed a real dislike of women and had no interest in dating anyone anytime soon.

As he pulled into the Crystal Cove campground, Kyle noticed Aaron doing some work on the small miniature golf course they'd installed about nine months ago.

"Hey, bro!" Kyle called out to Aaron as he walked toward the third hole on the golf course.

"Hey, man," Aaron said as he waved his brother over.

"Whatcha doing?" Kyle asked as he shook his brother's hand.

"We had a little mishap with a sick kid. Trying to

clean vomit out of green carpet is not so easy. Or pleasant," he said with a laugh.

"Don't you have a cleaning guy that does this stuff?"

"Yeah. Paul. But, he's out of town this week. Lucky me," Aaron said shaking his head. "Ready for some lunch?"

"I'm starving. Let's go," Kyle said as he and Aaron made their way back to the campground's lodge. Made to resemble a log home from the mountains, the lodge was a popular spot for campers who wanted a good meal and reasonable prices. Aaron had come up with the idea right before he took over from the previous manager, and the lodge had become a moneymaker for the business.

The two men ordered their food from Betty Sue, the resident lodge waitress, and relaxed into the oversized log sewn chairs.

"So, what's been going on with you?" Aaron asked his older brother.

"Well, I told Mom this morning."

"How'd she take it?"

"Perfect, as we both knew she would," Kyle said with a smile.

"Yep, we lucked out in the mother department," Aaron said holding his glass of sweet tea up as if to toast his mother.

"That we did. So, how are things going with you,

baby brother?" Kyle asked, as he looked outside, careful to avoid eye contact with Aaron.

"Nice try."

"Seriously, man. I'm worried about you…"

"Well, don't be. I'm fine. It's just going to take some time, that's all."

"I know you really loved Natalie, Aaron. It's okay to grieve that loss," Kyle said looking at his brother.

"She cheated on me, Kyle. Why would I grieve losing a woman like that?"

"Because you dated her for three years and had a future planned with her."

"Well, it's over now," Aaron said shifting uncomfortably in his chair.

"Do you want to talk about it?"

"When were you elected the Dr. Phil of our family?" Aaron asked with a wry smile.

"Point taken. But if you want to talk, you know you can always come to me," Kyle said putting his napkin in his lap as Betty Sue brought their lunch.

"I understand that I'm behind, but isn't there any way to hold off on the foreclosure for another couple of months? I might be able to get enough extra hours… Yes, I understand it's been five months… So there's no way that I can get some help to catch things up?"

THE ONE FOR ME

Jenna begged and pleaded with the representative from her mortgage company, but they were no help. She'd called them at least once a week for months now, but she didn't qualify for any plans that would help her catch the mortgage up.

When her sorry ex-husband had run out on her and her daughter to be with a hot, young nurse at his hospital, Jenna had been left holding the bag. The house was in her name, and there was no way she could pay for it alone. It wasn't a huge home, but it was nice for the area. With a rocking chair front porch and a view of the ocean across the street, it was her dream home. She had wanted to raise Kaitlyn there and show her all that life had to offer. Now, she'd be lucky to find a studio apartment in some rough area of town.

Jenna put her head down on the cold, wooden kitchen table and sighed. She was all out of tears after her normal morning crying session, but her stomach churned with acid as she thought about telling her daughter that they had to move soon. Kaitlyn loved their home. From her frilly pink room to the fenced backyard, that little girl adored where they lived.

Not only was her best friend, Lila, right next door, but her school was just a block away. In fact, Jenna walked her to school each day before leaving for her first shift at the diner. Today, there were no hours to be had, so Jenna was stuck at home trying to figure a way out of her tight jam.

She sat up and looked around her kitchen, remembering all of the work she'd done to make it perfect. The beach theme was subtle with sea foam green walls and stark white cabinets. She didn't want it to look like a vacation home, but she wanted to bring the ocean colors indoors. Her eyes scanned the walls, the counters, the small accessories she'd bought, trying to etch them into her mind for the day when she wouldn't have them anymore. She tried to avoid looking at the stack of mail on the breakfast bar. She could see the bright pink late notices peeking through the clear plastic windows of the envelopes. No need reading those late notices, as she didn't have the money to pay them anyway.

Jenna had long ago given up on a lot of things. Given up on having a healthy marriage. Given up on having a stable home for Kaitlyn. Given up on ever being in love with a man who put her first. Given up on being able to earn enough money to keep her dream home from foreclosure. She was just getting by day to day, putting one foot in front of the other when what she really wanted to do was curl up in a ball wearing her comfy yoga pants. She wanted to hide in her bedroom, lose all responsibilities in her life and just be still. Quiet. Peaceful. But that wasn't to be. She knew at any moment, her home was going to be taken from her and there wasn't a darn thing she could do about it.

Her sorry ex-husband had only given her two real gifts during their marriage. One was Kaitlyn. The other was agreeing to allow her to buy a home in Ridge Cliff, a small town outside of January Cove. While Jenna would love to have lived back in her hometown, she knew that prancing around with her husband and child in front of her ex and his family wasn't right. She'd broken his heart, and he would never have wanted to see her again. So, she moved far enough away to not be a burden in his life, yet close enough to enjoy the beach that she loved so much.

In her effort to stay out of the limelight, she'd started going by the name J.A. Watson, using her initials and her married last name. She didn't want to be found by anyone from her previous life, especially not now that she was a washed up single mother, wannabe artist whose house was being foreclosed on.

CHAPTER 3

A lot of Kyle's day was made up of knocking doors and looking for homeowners who were in trouble. His bread-and-butter was finding people who were behind on their mortgage payments and needed him to bail them out. Then, he would pay that past due balance and take over ownership of the property allowing the homeowner to avoid getting a foreclosure on their credit report. The homeowner would move out immediately, and he would have a property to fix up and flip or lease out to a tenant.

Of course, sometimes he purchased properties through real estate agents who had foreclosures listed. Other times, he worked directly with the bank to get them to sell the house for less than the payoff. One thing was for certain; Kyle was a whiz kid when it came to real estate investment properties.

On the flipside of that, he'd had to learn to be non-emotional about it. Homeowners could be in trouble for a variety of reasons from divorce to death, but he couldn't get tied up in that part of it. He had to look only at the numbers. That was the only way to survive in the real estate investing business.

Most of the time, he just knocked the doors around January Cove, but he was finding that it was a limited supply of properties for him. If he was ever going to grow his business, he had to get out into some of the outlying areas around January Cove. For that reason, he also hired a bird dog. This was someone who sought out investment opportunities and then passed those leads along to Kyle. If he closed on one of them, he paid the bird dog a fee. Sometimes, his bird dogs found him the best leads because they were out driving around in the surrounding areas that Kyle couldn't always get to.

The worst part about knocking doors was that he often ran into very angry homeowners who were losing their houses. Maybe they didn't know that their home was in foreclosure or they were trying to deny it, and he would have to walk up to their door and face them. Often, this could lead to a confrontation that Kyle didn't want. If the person wasn't interested in his help, that was fine with him. He didn't have any interest getting into an argument about it, however. Even though he had to lack emotion about the deal, the homeowners couldn't do that. They always had emotions whether they felt sad, angry or desperate.

On this particular morning, he was becoming more and more frustrated by the people he was encountering. Everyone seemed to be mad on this particular Tuesday morning, so he decided to stop into his favorite coffee shop and take a break. As he walked in, he heard a high-pitched squeal from across the room as a woman came running to him and threw her arms around his neck.

"Kyle Parker!" the woman said with a big grin on her face. He only vaguely recognized her, so he must've looked very confused. "You don't remember who I am?"

"Actually, you look familiar…"

"Sylvia Turner. We went to high school together. Remember?"

"Oh, Sylvia, of course I remember." He didn't remember her at all, but he didn't want to hurt her feelings.

Kyle had been very popular in high school playing on the baseball team and working in the student council. A lot of people knew him that he didn't necessarily know. But, he learned one thing from his mother. Always be nice to people whether you like them or not. And this applied. He didn't know if he liked this person or not, but he was going to make her feel like he remembered her nonetheless.

"I just stopped back in town to see my parents, and I've enjoyed seeing some of my old high school friends here, too. I had no idea you were still here. I figured you and Jenna moved away from January Cove a long time ago," she said still grinning from ear to ear.

Kyle looked down at his shoes for a moment and tried to gather himself. It'd been a while since he had heard Jenna's name spoken by anyone, although he thought about her every day of his life. His soul stirred at the mention, but he quickly regained his composure and took a deep breath.

"Oh, I'm sorry. Did I say something wrong?"

"No, it's fine. Jenna and I broke up many years ago. She actually met someone in college and married him, I believe. I haven't seen or spoken to her in a long time."

"I'm so sorry to hear that. I had no idea. I always assumed that you two would live happily ever after because you were such a great couple. I'm sorry to hear that things didn't work out."

A moment later, the woman behind the counter called out Sylvia's name and handed her a coffee cup.

"Well, I better go. I'm going shopping in town with my mother today. It was so nice to see you again, Kyle," she said giving him a quick peck on the cheek before she walked out the front door.

Kyle took a deep breath before walking up to the counter to order his coffee. He didn't like to think about Jenna and what they'd had. And what he'd lost. It made him sad and angry at the same time. He would never forget what she'd done to him, and he'd never forgive her for it either.

As he picked up his coffee and found a seat, Kyle started looking over some paperwork. His phone rang, and he immediately recognized the number as Jimmy, one of his bird dogs.

"Hey, Jimbo," he said.

"Hey, Kyle. Listen, I've got a hot lead for you."

"Great, because I'm striking out all over the place today."

"This one is actually foreclosing on the courthouse steps today."

"It's foreclosing this morning?" Kyle asked.

"Yes. Sorry for the short notice, but it's outside of town. It's not in January Cove, but it looks like it might be a really good deal."

"Give me the address and I'll go take a look at the outside. If I like it, I'd love for you to go ahead and bid on it for me today at the courthouse. If we win it, I'll bring the money over before the end of the day."

When Kyle hung up the phone, he took the address and put it into his pants pocket and headed out the door. Jumping into his Jeep, he started the trip over to see the outside of the home. If he could get a good deal on it, he knew that he could resell it.

That was a great part of town, and he hadn't bought anything over there yet.

JENNA DECIDED to get up and get ready for the day. Although she didn't have any hours to work that day, she was volunteering at Kaitlyn's school. She got ready and began the walk to the elementary school. This was one part of her day that she looked forward to. The kids were going to be having a class party, and she was bringing the cupcakes. Thankfully, the ingredients were inexpensive and she and Kaitlyn had had a fun time decorating them last night.

As she walked into the school, she looked around at all the happy children with their moms and dads visiting. It was a day that parents could visit and eat lunch with their kids, and she hated the thought that her child wouldn't have that. Her child's father had no interest in being a father. It made Jenna mad at herself when she thought about it. How could she have missed all the signs that the man she was married to was a complete and total jerk?

She walked into Kaitlyn's class and saw her sitting at her desk, smiling and coloring as usual. She was so thankful that her daughter was resilient and seemed to be moving through the process of losing her family unit easily. Of course, she knew there would be fallout one day. One day, Kaitlyn might look back at her and wonder why she hadn't tried harder to save her marriage, her family.

"Mommy!" Kaitlyn called as she ran across the room and hugged her mother's legs.

"Hey, baby!" Jenna said with a big smile, hoping no one would notice her red, puffy eyes.

"I'm coloring a picture for you, so don't look," Kaitlyn said shaking her index finger at her mother.

"I won't look. I promise," Jenna said holding up her right hand.

"Hi, Jenna."

Jenna turned around to see Susan Keller, Kaitlyn's teacher, standing behind her.

"Oh, hi, Susan. How are you today?" Jenna asked forcing another big smile.

"Good. How are you doing?" Jenna could feel the sympathy in Susan's voice. She knew about Kaitlyn's father leaving them, and the concern in her voice was evident.

"I'm doing very well. Thanks for asking," Jenna said trying to avert her eyes from the older woman back to Kaitlyn.

"Mommy, don't look!" Kaitlyn chided. Jenna had no choice but to look back at the teacher.

"I'm glad to hear you're doing well. I've been a little... worried."

"Worried?" Jenna asked furrowing her eyebrows. "About me?"

"Well, yes, a little bit. But more about Kaitlyn."

"Why have you been worried about Kaitlyn?"

"She's said some things recently…"

"What has she said?"

Susan waved her over to a quiet corner of the room and pointed to a chair. Sitting across from Jenna, she shifted uncomfortably in her chair.

"I've hesitated telling you this because I don't want to add more stress to your life…"

"Please, tell me what my daughter has said." Jenna was growing more and more anxious.

"Last week, she drew a picture of her family, including her father. The kids were supposed to explain the picture to the class, as it was about all of the things we are grateful for in our lives. As she stood in front of the class, she explained that she was grateful for her mommy and then she tore the picture in half right in front of the class. She said her mommy and daddy broke up and that her daddy didn't love her anymore."

Jenna's heart sank. Apparently her daughter had been more affected by the breakup than she'd originally thought. But what was Jenna to say to her? That her Daddy did love her? It didn't seem to be true given the way he was ignoring her and not paying child support.

"Oh, my goodness," was all Jenna could manage to say.

"Unfortunately, there's more," Susan said looking at her hands.

"More?"

"Yes. Yesterday, we were building houses out of popsicle sticks..." she started. Jenna's stomach churned. Houses. She knew where this was going. "Kaitlyn refused to build one. When I asked her why, she said that she wasn't going to have a home soon. She said mommy cries everyday when she doesn't know I can hear her. She said she keeps asking the mean man on the phone if she can pay him later, but he says no. Then she started to cry, Jenna. We had to take her to the counselor's office because the other children were getting worried about her. That's why I wanted to talk to you about it today."

Jenna's eyes filled with tears as she tried to look away. Susan reached across and touched her hand. Jenna shook her head and pulled her hand away.

"I can't," she whispered. "I can't get upset."

Susan nodded and sat silently as Jenna pulled herself together.

"Okay, here's the truth. My jerk of an ex-husband left us without money. The house is in my name, and I think he planned that at the beginning. He isn't paying child support either, so we are in foreclosure. At this point, I don't know where we're going or what we will do. I thought Kaitlyn was oblivious to it because she never talks about it to me, but apparently she has picked it all up. She's so smart."

"Kids are much more observant than we give

them credit for sometimes," Susan said. "Is there anything I can do?"

"No. There's really nothing anyone can do."

"Do you have family that can take you in?"

"No. My family is all gone. It's just Kaitlyn and me now. And we will make it somehow."

"If my house was bigger…" Susan said.

Jenna smiled and shook her head. "Susan, I appreciate it, but this isn't your problem. I made a mistake years ago, and this is my payback."

"I don't understand."

"Never mind. Listen, can we keep this between us?"

"Of course."

"Great. Let's feed them some cupcakes," Jenna said regaining her smile and walking back toward the kids.

KYLE DROVE SLOWLY up the street looking for the foreclosure deal. The auction on the courthouse steps was in a little over an hour, and he needed to let Jimmy know whether or not to bid on it. Since it appeared that the seller was still living in the property, he decided not to walk in the yard or look in any windows. That was a good way to get shot in the South, so he opted to stay in his car.

From the outside, the home looked perfect. He

tried to imagine who these homeowners were as most people getting foreclosed didn't continue keeping up their home. This house appeared to be immaculate with light yellow paint and hunter green shutters. The garden in the front was perfectly manicured, and the yard was trimmed. The driveway was freshly power washed, and the windows were sparkling clean. He'd never seen a more perfect family home.

Facing the beach from across the two-lane road that led into town, the house was a great investment, no doubt. But Kyle couldn't help but feel bad for the owners losing it. Why would they continue to maintain a home so well if they were going to be put on the streets any day now?

He didn't know why that thought bothered him so much. Real estate investing had to be a numbers game. He couldn't be worried about someone else's bad luck or poor choices when it came to paying their mortgage.

"Jimbo? Yeah, listen, go ahead and bid on that house. What's the starting bid again? Uh huh... Okay, bid the starting bid and only go up about five grand more. Also, what's the owner's name?" Kyle asked as he ran through the plans with Jimmy. "J.A. Watson? Doesn't ring a bell. Alright, get back with me later and let me know if we got it."

Kyle took one last look at the house and then drove down the road toward January Cove. As he made the 20-minute drive, he thought about the name. Watson. He didn't know any Watsons. Of course, he rarely went that direction. People in January Cove tended to stay there since everything they needed was close by, including a beautiful beach and large shopping area.

As he heard his stomach rumble over the jazz music blaring on his stereo, Kyle decided to stop just outside of January Cove for an early lunch. He pulled into The Round Table, a small country restaurant that offered a great lunch buffet.

"Well, I'll be! If it ain't Kyle Parker!" he heard a booming female voice say from behind the counter. Kyle cringed a little when he realized Dolores Banks was working the lunch shift. It wasn't that he didn't like her, but she was the town gossip and her goal in life was to find out as much about the Parker's as possible so she could spread her version of the truth all over town.

"Hey there, Dolores," Kyle said, planting a fake smile on his face.

"How's that pretty mama of yours?"

"She's doing just fine," he said as he slid into a booth. Dolores slid in across from him, although it was hard given her non-petite frame. She shoved herself into the small space anyway; anything for some gossip.

"I heard about your poor brother, Aaron. He must be devastated over his breakup," she said, obviously digging for information. It was crazy that everyone in town knew Dolores was a gossip of epic proportions, yet people still told her stuff. Kyle would never understand it. "Have you talked to him?"

"Of course," Kyle said with a wry smile.

"Is he okay?" she continued to pry.

"Of course," Kyle said again, this time with a knowing grin.

"Anything I can do to help?" she asked with a forced look of concern on her face. Kyle leaned in slowly and waved his hand for her to come closer. He could smell her spearmint gum mixed with some kind of stinky perfume.

"You can stop gossiping about him." With that, Kyle stood up and got a plate from the buffet, piling it high with delectable Southern dishes as he smiled to himself. Out of the corner of his eye, he saw Dolores get up from the booth slowly, partly out of shock and partly out of her inability to pry her physique from the clutches of the small space, and walk back into the kitchen.

As he finished up his early lunch, his cell phone rang.

"Hey, boss. We got it," Jimmy said.

"Cool. How much?"

"Two thousand over."

"Not bad. Send the guys over to post a note. Schedule them for tomorrow morning to do the clean out. They need to touch base with me as soon as things are done."

Kyle had a crew of people that would post a note on the house letting the now-former owner know that the home had officially been foreclosed. Then, he would give the owner 24-hours to vacate, mainly for liability reasons, and have his cleaning crew remove any excess items.

Normally, homeowners were long gone by now. After getting late notices and a foreclosure notice four weeks before, they usually moved out before the home went to the courthouse steps. He couldn't figure out why this owner had stayed around, and maintained the property so well, but that wasn't his problem. He or she needed to get out... and fast.

CHAPTER 4

*a*fter spending the day with Kaitlyn at school, Jenna's spirits were starting to lift. Sure, a day with a bunch of elementary school kids wasn't going to change her situation, but she was happy for a respite from the constant barrage of scary thoughts entering her brain on a daily basis.

As they pulled out of the school parking lot, Kaitlyn requested ice cream. Although Jenna didn't really have the extra money to spare, she dug change out from the bottom of her purse and went by the local ice cream shop. They sat together as Kaitlyn recounted stories from school and ate chocolate ice cream with sprinkles on top.

Pulling in front of her house, she parked her car and watched as Kaitlyn immediately headed for the climbing tree in their front yard. The sun was starting to make its descent over the ocean, and

Jenna's heart broke at the thought of not waking up to see that beautiful ocean from her front porch.

Kaitlyn ran across the yard and up to the front door.

"Mommy, we have a note from someone. It's pink!" she yelled with delight. Jenna wasn't too fond of the color pink anymore. Kaitlyn met her at the top of the stairs and handed her the note.

Attention Homeowner: Your home was officially foreclosed this morning on the county courthouse steps. Our company has taken ownership of this property, and we will be taking possession within 24 hours. Please remove any property you plan to take with you to your new residence before noon tomorrow, as our clean-out crew will arrive at the property at that time. Thank you.

Jenna's breath felt like it was sucked out of her. She sank down onto the top step, holding her stomach like she'd been gut punched.

"Are you okay, Mommy?" Kaitlyn asked patting her mother on the head.

"Yes, honey. I'm just fine. Listen, why don't you run over to Lila's house for a few minutes and tell her about those cupcakes we ate today, okay? Tell her Mommy I will come get you in just a few minutes," she said as Kaitlyn bounced across the yard and into Lila's house.

Jenna struggled to get to her feet, feeling like the

life was drained out of her and she might just pass out. What on Earth was she going to do now?

She quickly unlocked the front door and sat down on her sofa, dialing the mortgage company's phone number on her cell phone. After confirming her account information, she was connected with a customer service representative.

"Yes, hello. This is J.A. Watson, and I received a strange notice on my door saying my home was foreclosed today?"

"Yes, ma'am. According to our records, your home was sold to an investor this morning."

Jenna struggled to hold back tears. "But I thought I had more time…"

"With all due respect, you had several months, Mrs. Watson."

"I know, but…" She took a deep breath. "Thanks," she said as she hung up. There was really nothing she could say. She didn't pay her house payment. She couldn't catch up in time no matter how many hours she had taken on.

"Everything okay, Jenna?" She heard a voice in her front doorway. It was Becca, Lila's mother from next door.

"Oh, Becca, I'm so sorry for sending Kaitlyn over unannounced. I've had some upsetting news, and I just didn't want her to see me," Jenna said standing up and wiping away a stray tear.

"What's going on?" Becca asked walking closer.

Jenna handed her the notice that had been posted on the door.

"Oh, Jenna... I had no idea you were going through all of this," Becca said with sorrow in her eyes.

"I know. I didn't tell anyone. I kept hoping I could get enough hours, but I could never catch up."

"What are you going to do? You only have until noon tomorrow?"

"Yes. And I have no idea what I'm going to do."

"Well, you and Kaitlyn can stay with us. Billy can move out of his room and..."

"No, I wouldn't hear of it, Becca. You just redecorated Billy's room, and that isn't fair to him."

"Then you'll take my office. I can always work from my laptop."

"Sweetie, I appreciate the offer, but this is my mess, and I have to handle it the best I can."

"Actually, this is Nick's mess," Becca fumed as she mentioned Jenna's ex.

"Part of it is, of course, but I should be able to take care of myself and my daughter as a grown woman."

"Jenna, you can't possibly blame yourself."

"I shouldn't have given up my life and dreams for my parents or Nick. If I'd just done what my heart was saying all those years ago..."

"Don't do that, girl. You can't regret things. Think of it this way, if you hadn't married Nick, you wouldn't have our sweet Kaitlyn," Becca said with a half-hearted smile as she put her hands on Jenna's shoulders. "I feel really bad to leave you here alone."

"Oh, that's right, you guys are leaving in the morning, aren't you?" Becca and her family were leaving for a week-long trip to see her parents in Colorado.

"You have full access to our house, okay?"

"Thanks," Jenna said with a smile, all the while knowing she would never go into Becca's house no matter what happened. She had too much pride for that. She wasn't going to let someone else clean up her mess.

"Can you do me a favor?"

"Sure."

"Give me about thirty minutes to get myself together and then send Kaitlyn back over."

"Will do. I'm so sorry, Jenna. I wish there was something I could do."

"Find Nick and kill him."

"Done," Becca said with a chuckle. "Consider it an early Christmas gift."

After Becca left, Jenna cleaned her face up and started cooking dinner. When Kaitlyn came home, she served her spaghetti and then started the process of explaining what was about to happen. Kaitlyn didn't seem to understand it well, but Jenna could only hope that she would roll with it the next day when they had to start packing up their belongings.

She put Kaitlyn in bed early and started packing her things into the boxes she'd kept in her garage for years. Thankfully, she had enough to pack up although she had no real way to transport them and no place to take them to. Tomorrow she would start calling apartment complexes to see if she could find a small studio apartment or even a one bedroom if she was lucky. Maybe she would end up in an extended stay hotel. Either way, she would make sure that she and Kaitlyn were fine.

As Jenna slid into bed that night, she was exhausted. The mental and emotional toll was hard enough, but now her body was tired from packing too. How would she ever get through this?

"Mommy?" she heard Kaitlyn's strained voice beside her in the dark, noticing the time on the clock was two in the morning.

"Kaitlyn, what's wrong?"

"I feel sick," she said through tears before vomiting right beside Jenna's bed.

"Oh, sweetie," Jenna said jumping up and picking her up. She carried her to the bathroom, putting a cold compress on her head. "You're burning up with fever."

Kaitlyn threw up again in the toilet and cried. Jenna rubbed her back and tried to calm her down. There had been a bad stomach virus going around, and it appeared that Kaitlyn had succumbed to it. Great. This was wonderful timing.

Jenna sat with Kaitlyn until four in the morning before she finally fell asleep. Her fever broke around five in the morning, when Jenna was able to doze off for a couple of hours. When she woke up, she was careful not to wake Kaitlyn as she started looking online for apartments. Every call she made was devastating to her. No availabilities. Rent too high. Too far from work. Rejection everywhere she looked.

Around nine, there was a knock at her door and she ran to stop the person from knocking before they woke Kaitlyn.

"Yes?" Jenna said pulling her robe tightly around her and running her fingers through her messed up hair. She knew she must have looked like death warmed over.

"J.A. Watson?"

"Who's asking?"

"Did you receive our notice that was posted yesterday?" Ah, it was the investor.

"Yes, late last night when I arrived home. I need more time. I..."

"I'm sorry, ma'am, but this is our normal protocol. Liability reasons force us to make sure that the previous owner is out of the house within twenty-four hours."

"Do you own this house now?" she asked.

"My boss does."

"And what is the name of your company?" she

asked, not sure why she wanted to know as it didn't matter.

"Emerald Investments." For a moment, Jenna was transported back in time. She and her high school boyfriend had loved to go to Emerald Cove, a small beach in January Cove. He'd said that he loved her green eyes so much, and Emerald Cove became "their place". And then she'd screwed up her life by making the dumbest decision she'd ever made. She gave up the man who loved her more than life itself and went for "stability." Where did that get her?

"Ma'am?"

"Sorry. I was just thinking. Can you please ask if I can have more time?"

"I really can't."

Jenna's anger started to well up inside of her like a raging river with nowhere to go. Why was the Universe or God or whatever doing this to her?

"I'm not leaving," she said without thinking.

"Excuse me?"

"My daughter is five years old. Her father left us here with nothing. She was up all night with a stomach virus and a fever. I've gotten like two hours of sleep. You don't want to mess with me right now. I've taken wonderful care of this house, and I'm not going to tear it down now that your boss owns it. You can tell him I will get out within the week, which is a more reasonable time, but I'm not leaving today."

"Ms. Watson, we are supposed to start cleaning this house out today. My boss needs to get it ready to resell."

"I don't give a rat's butt what your boss needs. If he wants me out, tell him to get his rich butt over here and remove me himself," she said as she slammed the door and locked it.

As she leaned against the door, she took a big breath and wondered what was about to happen next.

"HELLO?" Kyle said as he sat at his desk. Working from his home office, Kyle had started the morning in a bad way. The offer a buyer had made on one of his investment properties had been too low, another buyer's financing fell through and cost him time on the market and unnecessary hassle, and his dog, aptly named Cat, had sneaked out of the house, played in the ocean, and then rolled in the sand until he was so caked in it that Kyle had to bathe him outside. It wasn't the best start to a day, and he was in no mood for more bad news.

"Hey, boss," Oliver said. Oliver had been leading Kyle's cleaning crews since the beginning, and he was one of Kyle's most reliable workers. "Bad news."

"Lovely. That's just what I need today. What is it?"

Kyle snapped as he threw down his pen and ran his fingers through his thick, dark hair.

"The owner of your new property is refusing to leave."

"What? So call the police."

"Well, this is a unique case, boss."

"Oliver, they are all unique cases. Everyone has a story, an excuse, as to why they can't move out or why they couldn't pay their mortgage. I don't care about all of that. Call the police on him."

"It's a her."

Kyle paused for a moment. "It doesn't matter."

"She has a five year old daughter. Says she didn't get the notice until she got home last night and then her daughter was up all night throwing up with a fever."

"And you believe that?" Kyle asked shaking his head.

"Actually, I do. She looked pretty shaken up. She's asking for the rest of the week."

"No way. I've got workers lined up to get that house ready for sale. I can't let some kid throwing up mess up my plans."

"Kyle, you know I will do just about anything for you, man, but I'm not calling the police on a woman and her sick kid. Karma will bust my butt for that."

Kyle sighed and then laughed. "Fine. I don't want your butt to get busted. Tell ya what. Go ahead and leave, and I will run out there in a little bit to talk to her."

"Good luck, boss. She's a bit of a spitfire," Oliver said laughing.

"I've had my share of spitfires. I think I can handle her," Kyle said chuckling as he ended the call. One spitfire came to mind quickly, but he didn't like to think about her. No, she brought up painful memories of a young man standing in the road watching the love of his life choose another man. A richer man. A man with a better future. A man who would never have loved her like he did.

Kyle drove down the road ready to confront the unruly homeowner. He wished that people could just be civil and not cause him so much trouble. He paid his house payment, and he had a certain level of compassion for those in situations that weren't as stable as his, but investing was his business and this woman wasn't going to cause him grief.

He stepped out of his Jeep and walked up the cobblestone walkway to the front door. It was just after lunch, and his cleaning crew was waiting on standby for the phone call from Kyle. They were like Tasmanian devils moving through a property and getting it ready for renovations. Although this property didn't look like it needed much of anything from what he could tell. At least this would give him the ability to see inside a little bit, unless the woman came to the door with a shotgun or something.

Kyle knocked and put his hands in his pockets, turning to look at the beautiful ocean view. Yes, he thought to himself, this property will be a big seller. With dollar signs dancing in his head, he heard the front door lock click open. As he turned, nothing could have prepared him for what he saw.

Feeling like the air had been sucked from his lungs, he stood with his mouth gaping open in shock. Jenna. How could Jenna be standing in front of him all these years later? Was he at the wrong house? Maybe he wrote it down wrong.

She stood staring back at him, hollow eyes that were outlined in puffy redness from crying. Holding her hand to her heart, she attempted to speak but nothing came out.

"Jenna?" he said, barely able to conjure up more than a whisper.

"Kyle," she said, all at once sounding relieved and stunned.

"I don't understand. What are you doing here?"

"I live here. I own this house... well, at least I used to..." she mumbled with her eyes darting around in confusion.

"J.A. Watson," he said, more as a matter of fact than a question. "Ashley. Your middle name."

"I'm confused, Kyle. Why are you here?"

"Jenna, I'm the investor." He watched as she put two and two together in her mind. Her face went from shock to anger in a split second.

"You did this to me? What was this? Your way of getting revenge?" she seethed.

"What?"

"You bought this house and tried to kick me out so quickly because you hate me?"

"Of course not. Jeez, you know me better than that. Well, you used to, anyway. I had no idea you lived here."

"So this was just a coincidence? You expect me to believe that?" she asked with her hands on her hips.

By this point, Kyle had recovered from the shock and replaced it with his own version of anger. "I don't really care what you believe, Mrs. Watson. I'm here to inform you that you need to vacate *my* house before I have to call the cops on you." His teeth gritted, he did his best to avoid thinking back to those days when he loved Jenna more than anything on Earth. No, right now she was just another person in his way.

Jenna began to shake visibly before she broke out in sobs. She leaned against the doorframe for support before she started to slide to the floor. Kyle's heart started to pound as he realized what he'd just said to her. Call the cops on her? Sure, he was angry, but he would never have called the police to remove her. She was Jenna. His Jenna.

"Oh, God, Jenna. I'm so sorry. I didn't mean to upset you. Come on..." he said as he crouched and slid his arms under hers. One touch and he was taken back in time. Her skin, the smell of strawberries in her hair, her presence. He pulled her up and was taken by how womanly she looked with curves. She wasn't that young girl anymore, but she was better looking now than when they were younger.

He walked her to the sofa and then shut the front door. She pulled her knees up to her chest and wrapped her arms around herself. She'd always done that as a protection mechanism. As her sobs slowed down, she finally looked up at him. One moment of eye contact felt like a dagger in Kyle's heart.

"What happened, Jenna?" he asked softly as he sat across from her.

"Mommy?" Kaitlyn said as she rubbed her eyes and stumbled into the living room. Kyle was taken aback by how much she looked like Jenna. With her sun kissed auburn hair and bright green eyes, the little girl took his breath away for a moment.

"Hey, baby," Jenna said, jumping up and kneeling in front of the little girl. "How are you feeling?"

"Hungry," she said and Jenna laughed as she hugged her.

"That's a good sign," Jenna said as she felt her head. "No more fever. Let's go make you some toast. Kyle, I'll be right back," she said looking back at him. He nodded and watched her walk into the kitchen. As he listened to mother and daughter talk, he realized how long it had been. She was a mother now. Someone called Jenna "Mommy." How could that be?

Hadn't they just had their first kiss on the big rock at Emerald Cove? Didn't they just go to the prom, Jenna all fancied up in her pink dress?

A few minutes later, Jenna reappeared in the living room, now wearing a pair of tight fitting jeans and a V-neck t-shirt that showed off the changes in her now womanly body. Kyle's heart skipped, and he had to remind himself that he was there on business and she was only a part of his past.

"Sorry about that. She was so sick all night. I barely slept myself," she said running her fingers through her hair with a slight smile. He remembered running his fingers through her sweet smelling hair many times.

"You look..." he started to say beautiful without thinking.

"What?"

"Nothing. I was just going to say sorry she was sick." Jenna eyed him carefully for a moment, and he could almost sense a hint of a smile. Had she known what he was about to say?

"Thanks."

"So, tell me what happened, Jenna. When last I saw you, you were speeding off into a life of glitz and glamor and money. I never imagined we'd meet up again this way."

"Well, where do I even begin? I helped put Nick through medical school, supported him through residency, gave birth to his daughter, and then he repaid me by cheating with a nurse at his hospital and leaving us with nothing." Kyle struggled with his emotions, which were ranging from anger to some kind of "I told you so" feeling. Because he had told her so.

He'd stood with his hands in his pockets as Jenna stood across from him with her head down. "I don't understand, Jenna. We had plans. We were going to get married one day. I love you," he'd said to her. She couldn't look at him.

"I love you, too. You know that. But I have to do what's best for me, Kyle."

"You mean what's best for your parents. When are you going to live for yourself?" he'd asked her.

She sighed and looked up at the sky. "Why are you making this so hard?"

"Hard? Are you kidding me? Hard is when the love of your life comes home from college to visit and tells you that she's dating another guy because he can give her a better future. How do you think that makes me feel? Not only did you apparently cheat on me, but now you tell me I have no future?"

"Kyle, it's just that my Mom and Dad think I deserve more..."

"More? What kind of more, Jenna? More money? He might be able to provide that. But more love? More devotion? More loyalty? Not a chance. No man will ever be able to give you the love that I can. I've spent years loving you, and whether you believe it or not, I've left my mark. You'll see. He can't love you like I do, Jenna," he'd

said as he walked closer to her, his lips only inches from hers.

"Kyle, I..."

"Don't worry. I'm not going to kiss you. The next time I kiss you, I want you to crave it. I want you to know that I'm the only man for you. You know deep in your heart that this will never work. He's not your soul mate, Jenna. Your parents are about to ruin your life, but I'm not going to beg."

She had stepped back, unable to meet his gaze.

"I'm sorry. This is what I have to do. Don't wait for me," she'd said. "You need to move on with your life."

He hadn't said anything else as he watched as she drove out of sight and out of his life.

CHAPTER 5

"Kyle? Are you still with me?" Jenna asked looking at him.

"What? Oh, yeah. I was just thinking about something." Kyle didn't know how to feel. Should he kick her to the curb and laugh all the way home at the thought of her being homeless and sad? Should he scoop her up in his arms like he wanted to do? Of course not. That part of his life was long over, and he wasn't signing up for more hurt from Jenna.

"Thinking that you told me so?" she asked looking down at her lap. She'd changed so much over the years, but some things hadn't changed at all. The way her hair smelled, even from a few feet away. The way she looked down nervously when she thought someone was angry with her. He'd seen her do it with her parents many times. Even the way her voice lilted in that sweet Southern way that drew him to her in the first place.

"No. Of course not," he said, lying through his teeth.

"It's okay, Kyle. You have the right to gloat."

"Fine. You want me to gloat?" he said standing up, finally unable to hold back his words. "You left me standing there like I didn't even matter, Jenna. Like our five years together meant nothing to you. So, yes, there is a part of me that feels pretty vindicated in all of this. He might have money now, but you didn't get the benefit of that, did you?"

"I'm so sorry, Kyle. I should have handled it all better. I know that. I knew it the moment I drove away and saw your face in the rear view mirror. You didn't deserve that, and maybe that's why I'm being punished now."

Before Kyle could speak, the little girl came running into the room. Amazing how fast kids could bounce back from vomiting all night.

"Mommy, who is this man?" she asked as she tugged on Jenna's shirt.

"Honey, this is one of my oldest friends in the world, Mr. Parker."

"How old is he?" she asked with her eyes. Kyle let out a chuckle as Jenna tried not to crack up herself.

"No, sweetie, that just means I've known him for a long time. He's the same age as me, which is very young," Jenna said smiling.

"Oh."

"Kyle, this is my daughter Kaitlyn," Jenna said. The little girl looked up at him with her big green eyes and Kyle suddenly felt like the world's biggest jerk.

"Hi there, Kaitlyn. I'm Kyle. Nice to meet you. Are you feeling better?"

"Yep. Lots better. Going to play with my dolls now!" she said before she bounded up the stairs singing all the way.

"She has plenty of energy," Kyle said.

"Yes, she does," Jenna replied with a look of sadness on her face as she sat back down.

"When did he leave?"

"About eight months ago."

"I'm sorry you and Kaitlyn have had to go through that. I wouldn't wish a nasty breakup on my worst enemy," he said avoiding eye contact.

"Not even on the person who did the very same thing to you?"

Kyle cringed a bit at her statement and then didn't respond to it. "He doesn't pay any child support?"

"He's supposed to, but he hasn't so far. He's angry with me, and he doesn't want me to have any of his money even if it means his own daughter goes hungry, I suppose."

"Mad at you? Why? I thought he was the one who cheated on you."

57

"He did."

"So what is he mad about?"

"Never mind. It's not important now. Look, about the house..."

"Relax, Jenna. Even though you're probably my least favorite person in the world, I wouldn't put you and your daughter out in the street. I'm not that kind of man." He was lying; she wasn't his least favorite person in the world.

"That makes me sad."

"What does?" he asked.

"That I am your least favorite person in the world. I really screwed this up," she said standing up and looking out the window at the ocean. "You know, when we bought this house, Nick promised me that we'd spend our off days as a family picnicking on the beach. We never went on one picnic. Now I won't have the chance to do that with Kaitlyn."

"Jenna, you'll have plenty of chances to build memories with her even if they are without her father. I'm sure you'll meet someone one day who will be your real soul mate, and he can be a great father to her." It pained Kyle to say "soul mate" as they had talked so many times about how they were meant to be together forever.

"I had a soul mate," she whispered just loud enough for him to hear. Kyle's phone started ringing just in time to break the tension in the room.

"Sorry, I've got to take this," he said as he pushed the answer button. "Hello? Yeah. Tell him I want the holes patched on the main floor and that damaged wall in the guest room needs to be sheet-rocked again. Right. I'll see you guys in about an hour."

"You seem to be in high demand these days," Jenna said smiling as she watched him type something into his phone.

"I guess so."

"How's business?"

"Good. You know Mom has the real estate company. I worked as an agent with her for quite awhile before venturing out on my own a couple of years ago."

"I used to see your signs when I would pass through January Cove."

"You did?"

"Yes. I'm embarrassed to say that I dialed the number on the sign many times, but never hit send."

"You wanted to call me?"

"Of course. I've missed you. You were my best friend in the world, and now I'm your least favorite person on the planet. That's hard to digest," she said just as Kaitlyn came bounding down the stairs again.

"Mommy, can we get a puppy?" she asked out of the blue.

"No, sweetie. We're moving soon, and we can't have a puppy where we're going."

"We're moving? But I don't want to move out of

my house, Mommy!" she said as her eyes welled with tears.

"We will talk about this later, Kaitlyn." The little girl stomped back upstairs yelling the whole way about how she didn't want to move. Kyle felt horrible and realized he had to do something.

"Listen, Jenna, I don't want you guys to have to rush out of here. You've got enough stress on you as it is. There's not much that has to be done to get it ready for sale, so why don't you stay here for another week or two while my guys do the work?"

"Seriously? You would do that for me?"

"I would do it for Kaitlyn. She seems like a nice kid, and she's already had one man disappoint her. I'm not going to be the second one."

"Thanks," she said softly as she looked down at her feet. "I appreciate it more than you will ever know." Their eyes met for a long moment as the tension built between them, and Kyle knew that was his cue to leave.

"I've got to get back to work, but I'll have my guys get in touch to coordinate what they need to do for me."

"Oh... Okay..." she stammered as he walked toward the door. Kyle turned around.

"I meant what I said, Jenna. I wouldn't wish this on my worst enemy."

"I know." He walked down the stairs to his Jeep and sped away as Jenna closed the door.

. . .

JENNA WALKED across the room and sat down on the sofa trying to catch her breath from the shock of seeing Kyle again. He looked good, better than good. He looked strong and sexy and successful. He looked like everything she'd known he would be one day until her parents talked her out of being with him.

How could it have been a coincidence that the very person who bought her foreclosed home was Kyle? And yet she believed him when he said that he had nothing to do with it. After all, how could he have known that she was J.A. Watson?

A knock at her door startled her out of her dreamy thoughts. Had he come back? Would he sweep her into his arms, cover her with warm kisses and take her away from all of her problems?

"Hey, girl. How's Kaitlyn?" Becca said as Jenna swung the door open.

"Oh, it's you..." she said sounding let down.

"Gee, thanks," Becca said laughing.

"No, it's not what you think. Come on in. Kaitlyn is feeling much better. Back to her old self it seems."

"I just wanted to come by and check on you. See how you're doing after getting that note last night. Why haven't you started moving?" she asked as she looked around at the non-packed house.

"Well, that's quite a story," Jenna said with a slight

smile. For the next few minutes, she recounted the shocking visit from Kyle.

"Wait. Are we talking about soul mate Kyle? **The** Kyle that I've heard about for years?"

"The very same one. Only he hates me. He said I'm his least favorite person on the planet, but he will let me stay another week for Kaitlyn." Jenna frowned and stood to get a glass from the cabinet. "Care for some sweet tea?"

"No, thanks. So, let me get this straight. He's going to let you stay a week, but then you're getting the boot?"

"Yep. But at least it buys me some time. Maybe I can find a decent place that will take Kaitlyn and me. I don't make much at the diner, but surely I can find a studio apartment."

"Well, it is the busy season around here," Becca reminded her. The whole area was busy from spring through summer, and a lot of people came to the shore for months at a time, which made rental properties hard to come by.

"True. I just don't want to have to take Kaitlyn out of her school. She's had enough change and turmoil in the last few months."

"Still no word from Nick?"

"No. He doesn't care, Becca. It makes me sad. I just don't understand how a father, especially a financially stable one, could do this to his daughter. He's mad at me, but she doesn't deserve any of this."

"He's the one who cheated, Jenna."

"I know. But he blames that on me. I wasn't blameless in our marriage, and he says what I did was the same as cheating."

"Oh, please, what a cop out. You didn't cheat. That was..."

"Stupid dreaming, apparently," Jenna said finishing her sentence. She didn't like to talk about what she had done to contribute to wrecking her marriage, and she didn't like to admit that she never loved Nick in the first place.

"Well, I'd better get back. Let me know if you need help packing," she said hugging Jenna.

"Thanks."

KYLE DROVE his Jeep into January Cove and then pulled off the side of the road next to the beach. He remembered this place well. It was the first time he and Jenna kissed, on the big rock at Emerald Cove. The carnival had been set up in the square and they'd walked to get ice cream at The Big Dip before walking down the beach.

He remembered that she wore a red and white floral sundress with cowboy boots. She always wore pink tinted lip-gloss, and when he kissed her she tasted like cotton candy. Ever since their breakup, he'd had a hard time seeing cotton candy as it always conjured up images of her. Of them. Of what he'd lost. And the worst part was that he seemed to have no control over her leaving him that day so long ago. He'd struggled with maintaining control over his life since then.

He watched from his car as seagulls dove down and picked up random scraps of food left behind by tourists. The sights and sounds of the ocean were in his blood, and he could never imagine living anywhere else but January Cove. Of course, a few years ago he could've never imagined living his life without Jenna. But he had, and he would continue to do so. This was just a blip on the radar screen of life. He wouldn't get diverted off his path now. He wouldn't get sucked back in. No matter how incredibly sexy she still looked or how adorably cute her daughter was, he wasn't making that mistake again.

"Jenna? Are you serious?" Kyle had called his oldest brother, Jackson, for some guidance on what to do about the situation with Jenna. Of course, Jackson probably wasn't the best person to ask. He'd been so livid with Jenna's parents back then that he'd confronted her father about how they had treated Kyle.

"Yep. It was a shock to go to the door and see her standing there."

"How'd she look?"

"Beautiful, as always. Puffy red eyes from crying, but still gorgeous."

"Damn."

"I know. Not what I was hoping for. Why couldn't she be three-hundred pounds heavier and covered in acne?" Kyle asked laughing.

"Because you would've still loved her," Jackson said, which was the truth and Kyle knew it. "Man, you know how I feel about love, but you could never get over her."

"I'm over her," Kyle insisted.

"No, you're not."

"Shut up. You're not even here, Jackson. What do you know? You're all the way in Atlanta making the big bucks, Mr. Multi-Million Dollar Real Estate Agent," Kyle loved to jab at his brother.

"You know as well as I do that I might sell millions of dollars in houses every year, but I sure as hell don't make millions," Jackson said laughing.

"If you did, I'd expect a cut of that since I taught you everything you know."

"Whatever," Jackson said snorting. The two brothers were close, always competitive and continually arguing about something.

Being from such a large family, and not having a father for most of their lives, the Parker kids had learned to be close. They protected each other and their mother with a ferocity that wasn't seen in many families. When Jenna had left him standing at the end of their family's driveway, it had been his brother Jackson who'd helped him nurse his emotional wounds and get back to work. Although just a little older than Kyle, Jackson had been the man of the family.

"Man, I've gotta go. One of my sellers is calling and bitching about something," Jackson said gruffly. He owned a real estate company in Atlanta, and he won awards every year for his high sales volume. Jackson was hard driven and a staunch competitor to every agent in town. No one wanted to go up against him, and the agents in January Cove were probably happy to see him leave a few years ago when he went off in search of riches in the big city. No longer tied to January Cove out of the obligation of helping to raise kids, Jackson had finally gone to pursue his dreams.

Kyle hung up the phone and went back to his own paperwork, trying desperately to put the thought of Jenna, sitting in her bathrobe, out of his mind.

JENNA HAD SPENT all morning dialing numbers over and over. Her fingers were starting to ache from all the dialing. Every rental listing she called about was either already gone, too expensive or way outside of Kaitlyn's school district. Already three days into her week long extension from Kyle, and she was no closer to moving out than she had been the day he came by.

Her job at the diner was also dicey at the moment. Word had gotten around that she was foreclosed, and her boss was starting to act a little strange. Small town life could sure be a challenge sometimes, and gossip was the language most people spoke. She often longed for January Cove where everyone knew her, and she could feel like she belonged.

As she looked through the newspaper, she heard a noise coming from the kitchen. It got louder and louder as she approached the door, and that's when she realized that her dishwasher had somehow malfunctioned and there was water all over the hardwood floors.

"Oh, my gosh!" she yelled as she attempted to get over to the dishwasher. Water was filling up the kitchen floor fast. She slid across the floor trying to find the water shutoff, but to no avail.

"Jenna?" she heard Kyle's voice behind her.

"Kyle, help!" she yelped as she tried to get up. He slid across the floor on his feet, somehow not falling until he got right over to the cabinet door where the shutoff was. He fell onto his butt, yelled, "ouch," and managed to get the water shut off and the dishwasher door open.

Covered in water from head to toe, Jenna sat up

and hung her head. Before he could say anything, she started laughing and crying at the same time.

"What on Earth?" he said.

"I don't know. This is my life," she said throwing her hands in the air as he sat across from her in the same puddle of water. "How did you get in?"

"I heard you scream when I was at the door, so I, um..." he pointed behind them where she could see the door had been busted open.

"Sorry," she said. "I swear I've never had problems with the house before."

"Murphy's Law," he said with a quirk of a smile. "I'm used to it. Looks like we have a plumbing leak to fix... and a front door."

"You were worried about me?" she asked meeting his eyes with hers.

"Anytime I hear any woman scream, I try to help. No biggie."

It pained her to listen to him lump her in with "any woman." She used to be his only woman, the love of his life. Maybe he just didn't feel those things for her anymore. For a moment, she toyed with the idea of telling him how she was partially to blame for the ruin of her marriage and her small family, but there was no reason to. He hated her, or at least severely disliked her.

Kyle ambled up to his feet and held out a hand to her. She looked at it for a moment and remembered for a split second all those times in high school when she fell at the skating rink and that same hand hoisted her to her feet.

"Come on," he said, urging her to take his hand. He braced himself against the counter and she put her hand in his, but somehow his feet slipped from under him and he fell to the ground on his back. Jenna went with him and landed squarely on top of him, her ample breasts pressed against his rock solid chest muscles and her lips only inches from his. It was all she could do not to reach down and bite that full lower lip of his, as she had so many times before.

"Are you okay?" she whispered, worried that he'd hit his head or hurt his back. He took in a deep breath and closed his eyes as if he was willing away some memory.

"Yes. I'm okay," he said softly. For a moment in time, they both froze, neither of them attempting to move.

"Kyle, I..." she started to say, but he suddenly moved and started to sit up. The verdict was in — he wanted no part of her. And who could blame him? She'd left him high and dry without a reasonable explanation all those years ago. He'd be crazy to trust her again.

"Let's try this again," he said with a smile as he pulled her up and helped her into the living room. Jenna grabbed two towels so they could both dry off and then threw some across the kitchen floor, although it wasn't enough to clean up the water.

"I think I have one of those wet vac things in the garage," she said. "Will that work?"

"Yeah. Tell me where it is, and I'll get it," he said.

"Should be on the floor in the back right corner."

A few minutes later, Kyle was back in the house running the wet vac over the kitchen floor. She watched him in his form fitting jeans and his navy blue t-shirt and wondered if this is what being married to him would have been like. Mr. Fix It working on the house, making it into her dream home. Would they have had their own children? Would he have taken her on those much-promised picnics at the beach that Nick never took her on?

"I think it's all cleaned up. You got time for me to look at the leak?" he asked.

"Sure. My friend Becca is picking Kaitlyn up at school today, anyway. She lives next door, and Kaitlyn is spending the night. So, I've got all the time in the world." She was secretly hoping he would stay longer knowing that.

"Great. Let me go look in that toolbox in the garage and see if I have anything I need," he said walking past her.

When he came back inside, he stopped and looked at her.

"What?" she asked.

"Don't you want to change into dry clothes? You're drenched," he said laughing as he reached out and squeezed some excess water from the front of her shirt. She shivered as soon as he touched her, and she was sure he noticed because his breath caught and pulled his hand back quickly.

"Right. Yes. I'll be back," she said as she backed up toward the stairs.

CHAPTER 6

*K*yle certainly hadn't expected this today. He was just stopping by to check on Jenna's progress of moving out so he could schedule his rehab guys. When he found her screaming and sprawled out on the wet kitchen floor, all he could think about was rescuing her. Hearing her scream was terrifying for him. What if someone was inside hurting her, taking advantage of her? What if her sorry ex-husband had come back to do her harm? Several scenarios had run through his head all at once, and the only reasonable answer he could come up with at the time was to bust the door down like some action movie hero.

But he wasn't her hero. He was her ex, too. And now he was her temporary landlord. He couldn't let this go any further, which was why he sat straight up when she landed on him on that wet kitchen floor. All he'd wanted to do at the time was scoop her into his arms and kiss her passionately to make up for all those years apart. He wondered how so many years could have passed yet it seemed like just an instant when he looked at her.

"All dry," she said softly as she reappeared in the kitchen where Kyle was working to fix the leak.

"Good," he said as he sat up and pulled his shirt over his head. "Mind running this through the dryer for me?"

He swore that he heard her breath hitch before she smiled and took the shirt from his hand. "S...Sure," she stammered. He didn't know why it made him happy to think that he was making her uncomfortable. Was it some kind of revenge? Was he hoping that she'd be sorry for leaving him all those years ago, looking like a fool at the end of his own driveway?

"So, how's the apartment hunting going?" he asked when she returned to the kitchen and sat down across the room at the breakfast table.

"Not very good. Every place I call on is either full for the season or too expensive. A couple were in horrible parts of town, and with Kaitlyn I just can't chance that."

"You've tried looking in Carter's Creek and Millhaven?" he asked, referring to two of the largest apartment complexes in the whole area. He knew they'd be the most likely places to find an apartment even in the busy season.

"Yes. Neither has an opening until at least late August."

"Yikes. That's almost four months from now..." Kyle said.

"Don't worry. I'll keep trying. I know you can't let us stay here forever," she said softly.

Kyle sat up and looked at her. "No, I can't. I have to pay some pretty hefty payments on this place because I used a short-term private loan. I need to flip it sooner rather than later. If I'd have known it was you and your daughter..."

"I understand, Kyle. It's not your fault. In fact, all of this is my fault."

He looked at her for a moment before the tension in the air was too much for him at which point he laid back down and continued fixing the plumbing leak.

"I'll go check on your shirt," she said quietly as she left the room. Kyle's phone rang on the table, so he stood to answer it.

"Hello?"

"Kyle. Thank God I found you!" Aaron said, his tone frightened and breathless.

"Aaron, what's wrong?" Kyle asked as Jenna returned to the kitchen holding his shirt.

"It's Mom. She collapsed at the office. They've

transported her by ambulance to Cove Medical Center."

"I'm on my way. Call Jackson so he can start heading in from Atlanta too."

"Already done. Hurry," Aaron said before hanging up.

"It's my mother. I have to go," he said taking the shirt from her and shoving his phone back in his pocket.

"Can I go? Please?" Kyle looked at her for a moment, but there was no time to argue. "You know how I love your mother, Kyle."

He knew that was true. Adele and Jenna had been very close, and it had broken Adele's heart when Jenna left almost as much as it had broken Kyle's.

"Come on. I don't have time to argue," he said, secretly thankful that he wouldn't have to go through this alone.

KYLE AND JENNA ran to his Jeep and drove in silence for the first few miles. Cove Medical Center was only about 15 miles away, but it seemed like hours. The thought of Adele collapsing was overwhelming for Jenna. It'd been so many years since they'd seen each other, and Adele had been like a mother to her. A non-critical mother. She prayed over and over in her head that Adele would be okay. Please, God, please.

"She's going to be okay, Kyle," Jenna said reaching over and putting her hand on top of his. He didn't move immediately, but eventually reached up for the steering wheel.

"I know she is. She has to be. She's a fighter."

"That she is."

As they pulled into the parking lot, Jenna's stomach churned. She had to be okay.

They ran into the emergency room and were met by Kyle's younger brothers Aaron and Brad.

"Kyle. Thank God you made it here," Aaron said.

"Where is she?"

"They're still examining her. No word yet," Brad said. "Jenna?" he said with a confused look on his face. "When did you two get back together?"

"We're not together," Kyle said without a millisecond passing by. It was obvious to Jenna that he didn't want anyone to think they were back together. "It's a long story. I just ran into her recently."

"Oh," Brad said, his face looking unsure of the story. "Hi, Jenna."

"Hi, guys. It's so nice to see you both. I sure wish the circumstances were better, though." She stared at the ground not knowing what to say. The last thing she wanted was to be the center of attention at a time like this.

"Are you Adele Parker's kids?" a nurse asked.

"Yes, we all are," Kyle said quickly. Jenna wasn't sure if he was trying to include her or was just so caught up in the moment that he forgot to exclude her. Either way, she was happy that she would be able to go back to the room with the men.

"You can come see her now, but please be sure to be quiet."

The nurse led them back to a room on the left. Adele was asleep, and she was hooked up to an EKG machine and what appeared to be fluids. The doctor walked in behind them and immediately ushered them into the hallway.

"I'm Dr. Clayton," he said shaking each of their hands. "Your mother is resting now."

"What happened?" Aaron asked.

"Well, a couple of things. It appears that she's had a stomach flu for a couple of days..."

"She has? She didn't tell me," Brad piped up.

"Me either," Aaron said as Kyle also shook his head.

"Well, her secretary said she worked right through it, according to the paramedics. Anyway, she was very dehydrated when she came in so we're giving her IV fluids."

"Thank God," Kyle said.

"But there's more," the doctor said in a whisper.

"More?" Aaron asked.

"Yes. Your mother's blood pressure was quite

high when she got here, especially for someone who is dehydrated. We did a few tests, and it appears that she might have suffered a mild stroke very recently."

"A stroke?" Brad said putting his hand over his mouth.

"Yes, sir. Thankfully, it was mild this time, but these kinds of things often lead to bigger and more serious issues if not treated properly. I'm going to recommend that she see a neurologist once she's feeling better, and maybe a cardiologist. It's likely that she'll need blood pressure medication as well as making some lifestyle changes to avoid a more serious stroke in the future."

Jenna eyed Kyle carefully, and she could tell he was feeling guilty about something. Amazing how someone's facial expressions can be so apparent to the person who loved them once.

"How long will she be here?" Kyle asked.

"Hopefully just a few hours until we get her hydrated again. Someone needs to tell your mother that she's not a spring chicken anymore. When she's sick, she needs to rest. This could have been much worse," the doctor said before walking off to answer a nurse's question.

The four of them quietly walked into Adele's room, and Kyle took his mother's hand. Her eyelids fluttered before she finally opened them and looked around the room.

"Is this a party?" she asked with a weak smile.

"If it is, it's a terrible one," Kyle said with a chuckle.

"I have a headache."

"I imagine so. You fell and bumped your head on the floor, Mama," Brad said coming around and taking her other hand. "And you scared us all to death."

"Sorry, my loves," she said before realizing Jenna was standing behind Kyle. "Oh, my goodness, is that you, Jenna?" A big smile spread across her face.

"Yes, ma'am. It's me." Jenna took a step forward.

"You're a sight for sore eyes! What are you doing here, sweetie?"

"Long story. I ran into Kyle recently. He just happened to be fixing a leak at my house when Aaron called him..." she tried to explain.

"You're a plumber now?" Brad asked with a quirk of a smile. Kyle rolled his eyes at his younger brother.

"Well, whatever the reason, I'm so glad you're here now." Her face looked tired. Actually, she looked completely exhausted, and it took a lot to wear Adele Parker out.

"Mama, why don't you get some sleep?" Aaron suggested as he made eye contact with his siblings.

"Yes, I'm quite tired," she said barely holding her eyes open.

The four of them left the room. Brad called Jackson to update him as he made his way from

Atlanta while Aaron walked off to call their only sister, Addison, who was on vacation with her husband in France.

"Want some coffee?" Kyle asked Jenna who nodded. They made their way to a small snack room off the emergency room hallway. Kyle took his coffee black, as usual, while Jenna loaded hers with cream and sugar. He'd always said her coffee tasted like syrup.

"I'm glad Adele is going to be okay."

"I'm not sure she is," Kyle said sitting down with a sigh.

"What do you mean? The doctor said..."

"I know what the doctor said, but I know my mother better than most anyone. I've never seen her look so fragile, so..."

"Human?" Jenna asked with a knowing smile on her face. Kyle looked down at his shoes. "Kyle, she's getting older. We all are. It happens."

"You know, I never got the chance to ask you where your parents are these days?"

"My mother passed away three years ago. Cancer," she said.

"I'm sorry."

"It was tough. She was only sick for a few months, but they just caught it too late. The chemo did nothing but make her sick."

"Cancer sucks," Kyle said shaking his head.

"Yeah, it sucks," Jenna said. "My father is still

alive, but he developed early onset Alzheimer's around the time that Mom got ill. He couldn't care for her really, so we had to put him into a memory care facility. He doesn't know me at all now, and he wasn't able to attend my mother's funeral."

"My God, Jenna. I'm so sorry. You've had the weight of the world on your shoulders these last few years," Kyle said with his eyes wide. For the first time, she felt like the old Kyle was in her presence.

"Yes, it's been tough. And then to lose my marriage and devastate my daughter and lose my home... Enough's enough. I'm looking forward to something good for a change."

Kyle nodded but she knew in the end that she was alone. All she had was her daughter, and that would have to be enough no matter how she longed for what she'd had with Kyle Parker all those years ago.

"How's your mother?" Jenna asked when Kyle arrived at her door the next morning. They'd stayed at the hospital for a few hours, but the doctor assured them there was nothing else they could do so Kyle had taken Jenna home.

"She's much better, thanks. We were able to take her home late last night, and she was feisty as ever, so I think she's on the mend. Listen, thanks for being there with me yesterday."

"You're welcome," Jenna said. "Come in."

"Where's Kaitlyn?"

"School."

"Right. I forgot it was Friday."

"Being at the hospital always messes up your week," she said. "Can I get you a cup of coffee?"

"No thanks. I just came by to check in on your progress with the moving," he said. He hated to push her, but the interest payments would kill him if he didn't get the house sold sooner rather than later.

"No luck yet. I don't know what we're going to do really. I did find out there is a shelter over in Crossville."

"A homeless shelter?" he asked with his mouth gaping open.

"Yes."

"Absolutely not!"

"Kyle, I have limited options here."

"Not that limited."

"Yes. They are that limited. I'm not like you. I don't have a big extended family that will take us in. We don't have anyone."

Kyle stared at her for a moment, his steely eyes cutting right through her.

"You have me," he whispered.

"Do I?" she whispered back. "Because the last time I checked, I was your least favorite person on Earth."

"Jenna..." he started but was interrupted by her phone ringing.

"Hello?" she said as she took it off the coffee table. "But, I don't understand. Why? You can't do this to me... I have a daughter to support..."

Kyle wondered who she was talking to, but he could definitely see that the conversation was not going well. Jenna's eyes were quickly filling with tears. She hung up and dropped her phone on the floor with her mouth hanging open. Sobs started to overtake her body, and Kyle helped her to the sofa.

"What's wrong?"

"I just got fired."

"What? Why?"

"She didn't really say, but I've been hearing rumors that they didn't like it when my home foreclosed. I guess they think I can't be trusted with money or something," she said, trying to take breaths in between her sobs.

"I'm sorry, Jenna," he said sitting down beside her.

"God, why is this happening to me?" she screamed as she stood up and turned her back to him. "Why? I don't understand! First, I lose my mother, my father forgets me, my husband leaves me, and I lose my house... Why? What is this for? Am I being punished?"

"Of course not, Jenna. You've just had some bad luck."

"It's not bad luck!" she yelled turning around. "It's you!"

"Me? What did I do?" he asked standing up.

"No, it's what I did to you. I'm being punished for leaving a good man behind without thinking. God is punishing me for hurting you..." she said, crying as she hung her head. "God, Kyle, you have to know I've regretted it every single day since I drove out of sight. I deserve all of this..."

"No, Jenna. You don't deserve any of this," he said softly as he walked forward and pulled her into his arms. Her face was pressed into his chest, which was wet from her tears within seconds. He could smell the strawberry scent emanating from her hair.

"Do you really hate me?"

"I never said I hated you."

"You said I was your least favorite person."

"Jeez, what are you, a tape recorder? Stop repeating that. I was angry at the time," he said. He continued holding her close to his chest. "The truth is, you were and will always be my favorite person on Earth, and that scares the crap out of me." The words had fallen out of his mouth before he could stop them.

Jenna's breath caught and she pulled back to look up at him. Kyle's eyes diverted to the side of the room. Making eye contact with Jenna was dangerous territory for him.

"I am?" she whispered, and he couldn't avoid looking into her deep green eyes.

"You are," he said softly. Jenna started to lean in to kiss him, but he let go and backed away.

"No, Jenna. We can't do this."

"I don't understand..."

"It took me years to get over you. Truth is, I never did fully get over you. I just learned to live without you. I can't ever do that again. It almost killed me. And as much as I would love to kiss you right now, I have to protect myself. It can't happen. I'm sorry."

"But, Kyle..."

"No. I'm sorry. I really am. But you're just an emotional wreck right now, Jenna. This isn't about loving me, as much as you might believe it is. Because if you'd really loved me, you would've stayed with me that day all those years ago. You loved Nick, and I am not in the business of being a replacement for another man."

"You don't understand, Kyle..."

"Jenna, I'm not trying to hurt you, but that part of my life is over. We can be friends, but nothing more. Ever. You understand?" She went silent, staring at him for a moment before she sat down.

"I understand," she whispered.

"Good. Now, let's figure out what to do next."

NEVER HAD Jenna felt more embarrassed than right now. He'd pushed her away this time and she supposed she deserved it. How could she expect him to ever love her again anyway? This was just part of her life sentence of being cast aside and unloved by everyone around her. Except Kaitlyn, the one shining light in her life.

"Are you listening to me?" Kyle asked as he waved his hand in front of Jenna's face.

"Oh, yes, sorry. I'm just a little tired today."

"I have a proposition for you."

"A proposition?"

"Yes. You and I both know that my mother needs to slow down for awhile, get her health under control."

"Of course."

"What if I hired you to be her assistant?"

"Her assistant? At home? She'd never go for that. She'd think you were hiring a nursemaid for her."

"No, not at home. I mean at the real estate office. You could be my eyes and ears, tell me when she's overdoing it. You see, I feel like some of this is my fault. I was there helping her run the place and then I left."

"Kyle, this isn't your fault. You're a grown man with dreams of his own. You had a right to pursue those dreams."

"Dreams don't always work out," he said softly, reminding her that she was once a dream of his.

"That's true. So what would I be doing?"

"Helping her with her schedule, paperwork, stuff like that."

"But doesn't she have a secretary?"

"Yes, but her secretary helps the agents and answers phones. You would be her personal assistant. She's never had one, but she needs one now. What do you think?"

"I would love to work with Adele, you know that. But I have some concerns."

"Such as?"

"Well, first I still don't have anywhere to live."

"I've been thinking about that, too. What do you think about you and Kaitlyn coming to live with me?"

Jenna's lungs seemed to go empty as she let out a cough to restart her breathing. Did he just ask her to move in?

"What?"

"Well, I figure we've already had the talk about never getting back together, so what harm is there in letting you live with me during the busy season? Once August rolls around and the tourists start leaving, you'll have saved plenty of money to find a new place. Of course, you'd have to move Kaitlyn's school and all, but I don't see how that can be helped really."

"Kyle, are you sure you've thought this through? I don't want to be a burden on you. I don't want to make things uncomfortable."

"It'll be like we're roommates, Jenna. That's all."

Jenna stood and walked to the window. "So many dreams we had for this place, and they're all as good as washed away in that ocean out there. Now I have to take the kindness of people who used to love me just to survive. It's humbling."

"I'm sorry your dreams got washed away, but sometimes we just have to start over whether we like it or not. We don't always get a choice in the matter." She knew what he meant.

"Do you think Adele will be okay with this?"

"Of course she will. She loves you."

"You think so?" she asked turning and looking at him.

"You have to ask?" he responded with a smile. "She always seemed to love you more than she loved me."

"Not possible." Jenna laughed. "But, I really would think she hated me for breaking your heart."

"She was disappointed, no doubt, but she never hates anyone." Jenna nodded in agreement. Adele Parker was a strong, good, loyal woman, and she wouldn't be able to find a better boss.

"Okay. I accept. As long as Adele is okay with it, so am I." Jenna smiled a grateful smile, and Kyle quickly looked away.

"Good. I'll go talk to her now. Maybe I can stop back by this evening and take you and Kaitlyn to dinner?" Jenna was shocked by the sudden invitation.

"Dinner?"

"Yes, it's the meal that one eats in the evening."

"Ha, ha very funny. I just didn't think..."

"Jenna, Kaitlyn needs to get to know me a bit before you guys move in with me, don't you think?"

"Oh, right, sure. Good thinking." For a moment, she'd thought he was asking her on a date.

"I'll be back around five," he said smiling as he walked out the front door.

Jenna slid into a chair and watched his car drive away. What on Earth had she just agreed to? And more importantly, what had Kyle agreed to?

CHAPTER 7

"*W*ell, Mother, I am shocked that you are giving me grief over this," Kyle said shaking his head.

"Not grief, darling. Just a warning. I hope you know what you're doing."

"What do you mean?" he asked, sitting down across from her.

"Kyle, this woman tore your heart out all those years ago. I watched you claw your way back to a normal life, and it took a long time. Surely you remember all of this," she said in her Southern drawl.

"Yes, I do, Mother."

"Why would you want to put yourself through that all over again?"

"It's just a job. We're not getting back together. I've explained that to Jenna."

"She and her child are going to be living with you, Kyle."

"And?"

"You don't think that's going to be very tempting?"

"I thought you liked Jenna."

"I adore Jenna! I fully expected her to be my daughter in law. But she broke your heart, Kyle, and I love you more. I just don't want to see you get your hopes up and something happens to tear you apart yet again."

"Mom, I promise that I am going into this arrangement with my eyes wide open this time. It's just about finding her a job to support her daughter and giving them shelter for a few weeks. That's it. Now, are you in agreement about giving her a job?"

"Of course. Whatever I need to do."

"Good. So, how are you feeling today?"

"Still pretty tired and worn down. Glad to be home, though."

"You gave us all quite a scare. Where's Jackson?"

"He had to head out early this morning for a closing in Atlanta."

"Wow. That was a short stay."

"Yes. You know how Jackson loves the big city. January Cove has become too small for your older brother, I suppose." She smiled wearily, and Kyle knew it was time to go.

"Get some rest, Mama. I'll check in on you later."

"Kyle?"

"Yes?" he asked turning around at the door to her bedroom.

"Be careful."

"Careful of what?"

"Hold your heart close, son. Protect it, okay?"

"Don't worry, Mama, I will."

KAITLYN SAT ON HER BED, eyes full of tears, with her arms crossed in defiance.

"I will not, Mommy! I will not pack up my toys!" she said pursing her lips.

"Sweetie, I know this is hard for you," Jenna said trying to soothe her upset daughter.

"I can't leave Lila! We just started our own club and we were going to build a tree fort!"

"Honey, Lila will always be your friend no matter where you live."

"I don't want to move, Mommy! Please don't make me move!"

Jenna felt wracked with guilt inside. She knew all of these changes her daughter was going through were partly her fault. Sure, Nick had cheated on her, but what she had done had certainly contributed to it. Her daughter could never know that. She certainly wouldn't understand it.

"Kaitlyn, sometimes in life we have to do things

that we don't necessarily want to do. This is one of those times. Mommy doesn't want to move either, but some things have happened that have caused Mommy to have to move. I'm sorry, but we are going to move at the end of this week. You're my big girl, and I need your help packing up these things, okay?"

Kaitlyn wouldn't look at her mother. "Fine, but I'm going to hate the new place."

"I doubt that. Where we're going is near the beach too, and my friend Kyle will be there with us. So you'll have a lot of new adventures."

"I don't like him either."

"You don't know him, Kaitlyn."

"I don't want to know him."

"Well, you'd better be nice because he's coming to take us to dinner tonight."

"No!" Kaitlyn yelped and ran into the bathroom, closing the door behind her. Jenna sighed and wondered how in the world she was going to navigate this new storm in her life.

Her thoughts were interrupted by a knock at the door. Looking at the clock, she realized it was just before five.

"Hey," Kyle said, as he stood on the porch with his hands in his front pockets. Man, was he sexy at the end of the day with a little stubble along his jaw line.

"Hi."

"Everything okay?" he asked. He was always able to read her facial expressions.

"Not really. Kaitlyn is upset about all of this. She doesn't want to move, and it's all my fault. I feel like the world's worst parent."

"It's not your fault. It's your sorry ex husband's fault."

"Kyle, I have to tell..."

"It's also my fault for making you move. Jenna, if there was anything I could do to let you guys stay, I hope you know I would. It's just that I bought this place using private lending, and the interest rates are very high. Plus, I bought it with one of my partners so I didn't tie all of my own money up."

"Kyle, this isn't your fault or your responsibility. I don't blame you. I'm just thankful that you are helping us at all, given our history."

"Let's try not to think about it anymore today because I'm starving and it might ruin my appetite," he said smiling, causing Jenna to remember the wonderful sense of humor he always had.

"Okay. Let me go get Kaitlyn."

She walked upstairs and Kaitlyn was still sitting on her bed looking out the window.

"Honey, our friend Kyle is here. We're going to get some dinner, so come on downstairs."

He's not my friend," she snipped.

"Well, he is my friend and he's doing a kind thing by taking us to eat dinner, so come on."

"But..."

Jenna kicked into mom mode. "Kaitlyn, do not talk back to me anymore. I'm not having it. Get your shoes on and come downstairs, young lady, or you will be on restriction from TV the rest of the weekend."

Kaitlyn was not used to her mother talking to her that way, but she knew she was serious so she put on her flip-flops and huffed downstairs.

"Hi there, Kaitlyn," Kyle said as she stood at the bottom of the stairs with her arms crossed.

"Say hello to Mr. Parker, Kaitlyn," Jenna chided as she walked up behind her daughter.

"Hello."

Kyle smiled at Jenna. "She's having a moment," Jenna rolled her eyes.

"Got it. Ready to go?"

"Yes. I'm starving," Jenna said smiling as Kyle opened the door for them both. As she walked toward the car, he stopped and stood in the yard.

"Where are you going?" he asked.

"I thought we were going to dinner..."

"We are."

"We're walking?" she asked confused.

"Yep," he said as he pulled a big picnic basket from behind his vehicle.

"What's going on, Kyle?"

Kyle walked closer where only she could hear him. "Well, I figured what better way to get her to like her new landlord than fulfilling something that her father never did?"

Jenna put her hand over her heart and took a breath. "Kyle, you don't have to do this."

"Relax, woman. It's just a picnic on the beach. You live right across the street. Honestly, I don't know why you haven't done this yourself."

"I don't know why really. I guess I always felt like it wasn't enough for her to just have a picnic with me," she said softly.

"Well, now she has me, too. And I'm super cool," he said grinning that schoolboy grin that stole her heart so many years ago.

The three of them walked across the road onto the beach. No one was there, as this stretch of beach was mainly used by the locals and not the tourists, and most people were further down the beach. Kaitlyn said nothing as they walked onto the warm sand.

"How about over here?" Kyle asked pointing to a spot.

"Looks good to me," Jenna said smiling. She marveled at how they felt like a family already, but she quickly brushed those thoughts aside. He'd been very clear about where they stood, and she had to abide by that.

Kyle opened the picnic basket and spread a red and white blanket across the sand. "Have a seat, everyone." Kaitlyn continued staring at the water as she sat down. "Miss Kaitlyn, I know you are not happy about moving. That would really stink. I think you should do your best to frown about it as much as possible." Kaitlyn shot a look at him that was irritation mixed with confusion.

"You do?" she said.

"Oh, yeah, for sure. The more you frown, the more friends you'll make."

Jenna stared at Kyle, unsure of where he was going with this conversation.

"I will?"

"Of course. People love to see others who frown. Don't you like seeing sad, angry people?"

"No..." she stammered.

"Oh. You don't? Maybe I'm wrong then," he said quirking his lip up.

"You're wrong. I don't like sad, angry people. My friends all smile."

"Well, then, you'd better turn that frown upside down, as they say," he said with a smile. "And I think I know just how to do that."

"How?"

"It's my super duper, out of this world, amazingly delicious 'Kyle's the Man' cupcakes!" he said as he pulled a tray of pink fluffy cupcakes from the picnic basket. Kaitlyn's eyes lit up like a Christmas tree. "See these sprinkles?"

"Yeah," she said licking her lips and trying to avoid a smile.

"Well, these are my special happy sprinkles that make people smile. I've never fed them to anyone who didn't smile after eating one, but you have to be careful."

"Why?"

"Because they are so powerful that they might make you feel happy about moving, and we wouldn't want that would we?"

"Well..."

"Wait. You mean that you might actually want to feel happy about moving? I mean maybe you could think of it as an adventure?"

"Maybe," she said, sitting back and crossing her arms. "I do like adventures." Jenna was quiet watching the exchange in awe.

"I have adventures at my house all the time."

"You do?" she asked with her eyes wide.

"I do. You see, I also live on the beach only there is no road between my house and the water. Your bedroom will have its own balcony just like a princess. And, if you get up early enough, you'll see Snickers."

"Who's Snickers?"

"My dolphin."

Kaitlyn couldn't contain her grin this time. "You have your own dolphin?"

"Actually, he's just my favorite, but I know his whole family. There's Snickers, Jumper, Flipper and Bob."

"Bob?" Jenna said under her breath with a smile.

"Yes, Bob, thank you very much," he said with a proud grin. "His real name is Robert, but we don't like to be too formal." Jenna could barely contain her laughter. Kyle had always been funny and outgoing and adventurous. He'd always been the one to act out in public just to get a laugh. It was a big part of what made her fall in love with him in the first place, and it was also a big reason why her parents disliked him so much. He wasn't mature enough in their eyes. She wondered what they'd think now that he was so financially stable and her ex had left her without a penny.

"Can I see Snickers?" Kaitlyn asked breaking Jenna's thought process.

"Well, that depends. You see, Snickers has two requirements for being his friend. One, you have to smile. He won't come around frowning people. They scare him. Two, you have to live at Parker Place."

"Where is Parker Place?" she asked.

"It's the house where I live, the one with the balcony. As long as you live there and have a big smile that Snickers can see all the way from the ocean, he will come around because he knows he can trust you."

"I can do that! I swear! Look!" she smiled as big as she could, showing off her almost toothless grin.

"That's pretty good, but I can barely see your back teeth," he said egging her on.

"How about this?" she asked with an even bigger grin.

"Oh, yes! That's it. I know Snickers will come around for that."

Yay!" she yelped as she sprang from her seat and jumped up and down. "Mommy, when can we move in?"

"In a few days, sweetie," Jenna said incredulous.

"Can I go look for seashells before we eat?" she asked. Jenna nodded as Kaitlyn ran off yelling, "woo hoo" all the way.

"Kyle Parker, you are one amazing man," she said shaking her head.

"Excuse me?"

"How on Earth did you manage to take a sad and angry little girl and turn her into your biggest fan in five minutes?"

"I think she is Snickers' biggest fan, not mine."

"Still, that was a miraculous thing to watch. Thank you."

"For what?"

"For making this easier on my little girl. She has been so devastated, and you just gave her something to look forward to. Oh, please tell me Snickers is real..." Jenna said with a look of terror in her eyes.

"He's real. I've had a family of dolphins swimming by my house for years now."

"Thank God," she said laughing. They sat for a

quiet moment watching Kaitlyn run through the surf and picking up seashells.

"Do you paint this?" he asked pointing to the ocean.

"I haven't painted since I met Nick, actually."

Kyle looked at her stunned. "What?"

"I haven't painted in many years, Kyle."

"Why?"

"Well, for one, my parents told me it was silly and not a real job. So, I ended up with a business degree I don't use."

"Still, you could have painted as a hobby."

"Painting requires inspiration, more than just a pretty scene to look at. For me, painting always had to be something that came from inside of my soul and had to burst out onto a canvas. I haven't felt my soul stirring in such a long time..." she trailed off and held back tears that were threatening to fall from her eyes.

"You should paint again. You were an amazing artist, Jenna, and people need to see that. Your parents were so wrong. You should do what you love in life."

"Sounds good in theory, but a single mother doesn't have the right or ability to do what she loves. She has to do what makes money. I'd do anything for that little girl right there," she said biting on her lower lip.

"I can see that. Okay, another question. How is your father?"

"Fading fast," she said as she watched Kaitlyn do cartwheels across the sand. "We started noticing his memory slipping when Mom was still alive, but no one wanted to face it. It finally became apparent that he could no longer take care of himself when he came up missing from home. We had to call the police and finally found him sleeping under the pier. He kept burning things in the kitchen, eating his cat's food... It was so sad. Crazy thing is that he has these moments where he remembers things from so long ago, yet he can't remember what he just ate or sometimes what my name is."

"I'm really sorry, Jenna. I know how much you love him."

"I do, but he's not in there anymore. My father is gone."

They sat silently again for a few moments watching Kaitlyn run around.

"Now my turn to ask a question."

"Okay, shoot."

"Did you date after I left?" Kyle froze in place for a moment.

"Of course I did. I had to move on."

"Anyone special?" she asked.

He sat there for a moment as if he was running through possible answers in his mind before speaking. "None as special as you were to me."

"Oh," she said trying not to smile.

"You ruined me, Jenna."

"What?"

"Ruined me for other women. No one ever compared to you, not even close. And I'm still looking," he said softly.

"I'm hungry!" Kaitlyn announced as she came running closer. The moment broken, Kyle gave Jenna a half-hearted smile as they dug into the fully packed picnic basket and started to eat.

CHAPTER 8

"*H*e said you ruined him?" Becca asked, with her mouth hanging open.

"Yep. Shocked me too."

"Then maybe you have a chance."

"No, I don't think so," Jenna said, wrapping a plate and putting it into one of her many moving boxes.

"Why?" Becca asked as she taped another box closed.

"For one thing, he told me that there could never be anything else between us."

"He could just be blowing smoke. Guys don't like for us to think that we have the upper hand," she said smiling.

"True, but if he ever found out how I contributed to breaking up my own family, he'd think I was a complete idiot. I mean, how desperate would he see me then?"

Becca stopped packing and looked up. "Seriously?"

"Yes. Seriously."

"Come on, Jenna. Nick did a lot worse."

"True, but maybe he wouldn't have if I..."

"Stop. You know Nick was never going to be faithful." Jenna nodded and looked back down at the plates she was packing.

"You got any wine?" Becca asked.

"Sure. Above the fridge," Jenna said pointing behind her.

Becca poured two glasses into red plastic cups. "I couldn't find any wine glasses," she said laughing as she handed the cup to Jenna.

"Already packed up," Jenna said. "You know, the crazy thing was how fantastic he was with Kaitlyn. She seems to adore him already, and that scares me."

"Why?"

"Because she's already lost her father, and now she's going to be getting closer to Kyle since we'll be living there. He's already made it clear that he doesn't want me in that way anymore. What if Kaitlyn gets attached and then he bails on her, too?"

"First of all, he does want you in that way, but he sounds terrified after the way you hurt him. Secondly, he doesn't seem like the kind of guy to bail on anyone. And third..."

"How many points are there?" Jenna asked chuckling.

"This one is the most important. Third, if you want to get him back, you'll have to make a plan. A good one."

"What makes you think I want him back?" Jenna asked, trying not to smile and give herself away.

"Oh, please. A stranger walking down Seabreeze Avenue could spot your lovesick face from a mile away!" Becca said throwing a balled up piece of newspaper across the room and hitting Jenna squarely on top of the head.

"Ouch!" she said, overreacting at the light piece of paper hitting her. "Okay, what kind of plan do you suggest?"

"One that makes him realize he is in danger of losing you all over again. Then he will either poop or get off the pot," she said nodding her head. Jenna had always hated that nasty sounding old Southern phrase, but it seemed to fit the occasion.

"First of all, gross. Second of all, how can I do that?"

"Duh, Jenna. Do I have to spell everything out for you?"

"Apparently."

"You have to find a good looking man who wants to wine and dine you a bit, and then you have to do your best to make Kyle jealous."

"That sounds very middle schoolish, Becca."

"Which explains why I had more boyfriends than you could shake a stick at in middle school," Becca said, grinning.

"Have you been reading some kind of Southern phrase dictionary?"

"I'll ignore that snide comment because I know you are lovesick and not thinking clearly," she said balling up another piece of newspaper. "Now, are you agreeing with my plan or do I need to execute another attack?"

Jenna sat for a moment and finally nodded. "Fine. I agree. But where do we find a man to wine and dine me that I won't hurt in the end?"

"I know just the man!" Becca said rubbing her hands together as she let out a ghoulish laugh. Jenna knew she was now in over her head.

KYLE SAT at his desk going over paperwork and looking out at the ocean. He'd been trying to go over numbers for two of his rehab homes for the last two hours, but all he could think about this morning was Jenna. Her smile. Her smell. Her voice. What kind of crazy plan had he come up with? Moving her and her adorable daughter into his house for a few months? Was he insane?

He already had their rooms ready and was just waiting for Jenna to finish packing. He'd stopped short of asking if she needed his help packing because he didn't want to give her the wrong idea. What was the wrong idea anyway?

Just as he was getting lost in thought again, his phone rang.

"Kyle Parker," he said gruffly into his phone.

"Good morning to you, too," Jenna said, her voice soft and sweet and everything he wanted to hear every morning for the rest of his life. Crap! Where did that come from?

"Oh, hey. Good morning, I mean," he said, stumbling over his words like a buffoon.

"I just wanted to tell you that my friend, Becca, came over last night and helped me get most of our stuff packed. I thought since Kaitlyn was at school all day, maybe I could bring a few boxes by? My car isn't very big, and I can't afford to hire a real mover."

"Sure. Actually, why don't you let me come over and fill up my Jeep, too?"

"Kyle, I know you're busy. I don't want to interfere..."

"You could never interfere, Jenna. I'd be happy to."

"Oh. Okay then. I'll be waiting," she said softly as she hung up. Good Lord, what was he doing to himself?

Kyle drove to Jenna's house with an unusual smile on his face. As much as he wanted to wipe it off, he couldn't help himself. Being near her again was making him feel whole. At the same time, he knew he couldn't let it go far. She was too dangerous to have in his life as more than a friend.

He pulled into her driveway as she opened the front door. She was loading a large box into the trunk of her small compact car. He jogged over to her and took one side of it.

"You should've waited for me. This is way too heavy," he said as he helped her slide it into the tight trunk space.

"I had it just fine, Kyle," she said trying not to smile. "Besides, a single mom has to learn to do things on her own. No one there to help."

"I'm here to help," he said softly as they walked toward the front door.

"I appreciate you saying that, but are you really?"

"What's that supposed to mean?" he asked, unnerved at her sudden independent streak.

"It means that I know you're trying to help us, and I am more grateful than you will ever know, but I'm the mother. I'm alone in raising my daughter. I'm responsible for her needs, her college fund, and her first car. So, as I see it, I need to start taking charge of our future."

"What brought this on?"

"Nothing brought it on. I've just realized that I can't sit here stewing about what could have been in my life. I have to start making some major changes."

"Like what?" he asked, unsure of if he wanted the answer.

"Well, for one, I can't be alone forever."

Kyle cocked his head at her in confusion.

"Let me just come right out and ask this, Kyle."

"Okay..."

"If we move in, are you going to be okay seeing me start dating again?" The words hit him like a ton of bricks. Here he was thinking he was rushing in to save the day, and she was thinking about finding dates? Had he been completely wrong about her?

Realizing she was waiting for an answer, he shrugged his shoulders as if not to care. "Of course. I date, so why shouldn't you?" he said, turning to pick up a box in hopes that she didn't see his face. He didn't date, at least not currently. He'd only been out with a handful of women in the many years since Jenna left him.

"Oh. I didn't realize..."

"You think I've lived as a monk since you left me, Jenna?" he asked staring at her for a moment.

"Of course not. Good, I'm glad we got that settled between us then," she said as she picked up another box and headed for the door.

JENNA DROVE her car behind Kyle's Jeep, cursing herself over and over again. What had she been thinking? The next time she saw Becca, she was going to smack her. No, strangle her. No, shoot her. Maybe she'd do all three for giving her that advice. Now she was further from ever getting Kyle back than ever. Why had she made that stupid remark about dating? She didn't want to date anyone!

"Hello?"

"Becca? I am going to kill you!" Jenna snapped as her friend answered the phone.

"Mom?" Becca said.

"Very funny. I took your stupid advice and told Kyle I wanted to start dating, and it backfired. Big time."

"How?"

"He said that was fine because he was already dating other people anyway."

"That's great!"

"How?" Jenna asked. "How is that great?"

"Because you took him off guard; kept him on his toes. Now he knows that you intend to move forward, so he's trying to save face."

"Or he really is dating someone and trying to warn me."

"Please. If he was dating someone, he would have never agreed to move you into his house." Jenna thought for a moment and realized her friend was more than likely right.

"So, you're saying that he just told me that because I shocked him?"

"Yep. Which means our plan is already working." Jenna had to smile at that.

"Alright, I'll hold off on killing you for a little while longer then," Jenna said laughing. "Oh, gotta go. We're pulling into his driveway now."

~

KYLE AND JENNA both got out of their cars at the same time, and Jenna walked toward him awaiting further instructions on what they were doing next.

"Before we unload, I'd like to show you around if you don't mind," he said pointing back at the house. "I wanted to show you your rooms so you can tell me if there is anything else you guys will need."

"Sure. I can't wait to see it. I've always loved this part of the beach," she said smiling. Of course she loved it because it was Emerald Cove.

Kyle walked up to the front door and unlocked it as he waved Jenna to go through in front of him. If there was one thing his mother had taught him and his brothers, it was how to be a Southern gentleman. And that meant always opening the door for a female. Before she could walk too far, a big chocolate lab came running toward her. He jumped up and kissed her right on the cheek.

Jenna laughed. "Sorry. This is my dog. His name is Cat," Kyle said smiling.

"You named your dog Cat?"

"I've always been a bit strange. You know that," he said pulling the dog down and telling him to sit. Jenna laughed and nodded as she walked further into the house.

"Oh, Kyle, this is beautiful!" she said as she walked into the living room. With its hardwood floors and soaring ceilings, she was amazed at how clean and modern it was. The walls were a sand color and there was a wall of windows looking out over the ocean.

She walked around as Kyle stood by silently watching her move across the room. He'd almost forgotten how she walked, with the grace of a ballet dancer but the enthusiasm of a child. She stopped and looked out the windows and put her hand over her mouth. Spinning around, she stared at Kyle and he knew in an instant that she remembered.

"Kyle, is this the place?"

"What place?" he asked, still trying to brush it off.

"You know what place. Right out there, by that big rock..." she said, pointing to the beach. Without waiting for an answer, she slipped off her shoes and walked through the French doors that led to a large white deck. She ran down the stairs and onto the beach with Kyle following her quietly.

Jenna made her way to a large rock that was being washed away over time, however slightly, by the crashing waves. She ran her hand along it as if she was looking for something, and when her fingers ran along the sharp edges facing the ocean, she found what she was looking for.

Kyle loves Jenna - Always & Forever

She traced the outlines of the letters slowly as her eyes welled with tears that she fought not to shed.

"Kyle," she said just loud enough where he could hear her over the sound of the waves.

He looked down at his feet. She walked closer and stood with her face only inches from his.

"Kyle, look at me, please," she said. When his eyes met hers, all he could see was the young girl he'd fallen in love with. "This house... how is it in the same spot where we had our first kiss?"

She was right, of course. The house sat on the exact spot where they'd shared their first kiss followed by many others. The rock was a spot where they'd kissed, carved their names and talked about life dreams. It was "their" place, and she'd remembered that.

"I could try to lie right now, but I'm not going to. When this house came up for sale, I had to buy it because I needed a way to remember you... us..."

Her eyes welled with tears. "That is quite possibly the sweetest thing I've ever heard anyone say."

"Don't get all sentimental, Jenna. It was years ago," he said, trying his best to brush it off and appear nonchalant. Inside, he was dying.

"Oh... I understand," she said looking very hurt

and trying to force a smile as she walked toward the house.

"Jenna, wait."

"Yes?"

"You were everything to me back then. I bought this house because it was the only link I had to you. I used to come down here everyday and sit on that rock and look out into the ocean. I would think about you, what you were doing at the time, where you might be. It was both heartbreaking and healing at the same time. Of course, I had no idea you were living so close for the last few years."

"Kyle, when did you buy this house?" she asked cocking her head.

"Why?" He knew why she was asking. He couldn't have possibly bought it right after they broke up. He was far too young back then and wouldn't have had the money.

"Just humor me. When did you buy it?" she asked, darting her eyes around.

Kyle leaned against the rock and stared at the blue sky. "I bought it six years ago."

Jenna covered her mouth with her hand. "Kyle, that was years after we broke up."

"I know. I wasn't getting over it, and this house came on the market as a fixer upper. It was my first real investment property. I learned a lot about the business from this house, just like I learned a lot about life from you," he said quietly, as he finally cracked a smile in her direction. Jenna sighed and leaned against the rock with him. "I never really understood why, Jenna."

"Why what?"

"Why you left me the way you did."

"Kyle, I was young and stupid. My parents were really pushing me to get out of January Cove and make something of my life. I was happy here, with you. You know how judgmental my parents were. My mother was pushing me everyday to find a successful man and get married. You know I didn't even get to major in art because she was so critical of the idea. When I met Nick, they were thrilled. He seemed more settled than you, and he was on the path to being a doctor. They saw that as my ticket to a life of wealth and success, and they started pushing hard. I've never told anyone this, but my mother threatened to cut me off from contact if I didn't drop you and date Nick, even though I'd told her time and again that I didn't think I could ever really love Nick."

Kyle stood there fuming inside. He'd despised her mother, but had never said so. Her father wasn't great either, but mainly because he went along with her mother. She was a force to be reckoned with and few people crossed her.

"After a while apart, I realized that the only way to protect you would be to do as she asked. If you and I had gotten married, she would've made your life miserable, and I couldn't do that to you."

"You know I would have done anything for you, Jenna. Even if it meant being around the wrath of your mother."

"I know, but I couldn't allow it. I wasn't going to watch her degrade you for years on end. She thought you'd never go anywhere just because you were raised by a single mother. Your outgoing personality scared her," Jenna said smiling half-heartedly. "When I think back now on all those years we lost and how weak I was, it makes me sick. But it is what it is, and I can't change any of it now."

"No, we can't go back again. What's done is done, but I've always wondered," Kyle said taking in a deep breath of the briny sea air. "Well, I should show you to your room."

"Kyle?" Jenna said as he started to walk toward the house.

"Yeah?" he said turning around.

"I'm so sorry I hurt you."

"I know," he said with a smile as he turned and continued to walk.

JENNA AND KYLE carted several boxes up to her room. As she unpacked a few of them into the dressers and closets, she looked out the window at the ocean and marveled at how some things never change. The sea never changes, and the feeling of something constant was what she needed. Stability.

With all her parents' efforts to make sure she was stable, they had failed. Now, she was as unstable as she'd ever been. Single motherhood. The one thing that her own mother was so critical about in Kyle's mother, and here she was in the same situation.

"Everything look okay?" Kyle asked standing in the doorway.

"Yeah."

"You alright?"

"I will be," she said with a smile as she returned her gaze to the ocean.

"Can I help?" he asked, obviously worried about her. He walked up behind her, and the scent of his cologne immediately carried her back to their days as a couple.

"No one can really help, Kyle. I was just thinking about the irony."

"Of what?"

"My mother didn't want me to date you, and one of the reasons was that your mom was a single mother. Now, here I am — a single mother. I bet she is rolling over in her grave." She chuckled softly, but it wasn't funny at all.

"Jenna, your mother loved you in her own weird way. She thought she knew best, but she didn't. Even parents make mistakes."

"I know. I just wish..."

"Don't do that. Some things can never be changed."

He put his hands on her shoulders and kissed the top of her head, a gesture that both shocked and comforted her. She wanted to turn around and fall into his embrace and erase all the years that had pulled them apart. Instead, she stood still, careful not to scare him away. He was like a timid dog that had been kicked by its owner, and she knew that coming on too strong would be a sure recipe for disaster.

"What time is it?" she finally asked after a few moments.

"It's eleven o'clock," he said looking at his watch.

"Oh, crap!" she said, as she started scurrying around looking for her keys.

"What's wrong?" he asked following her as she ran down the stairs.

"I'm supposed to go see my Dad and have lunch with him," she said as she grabbed her purse and opened the front door.

"Mind if I tag along?" Kyle asked, which stopped Jenna in her tracks on the sidewalk.

"You want to see my Dad?" she asked with her mouth gaping open.

"I actually liked your Dad... a little bit anyway," he said with a smile that made her insides melt. His dimples seemed to have deepened over the years, and she wanted to bite one of them right now.

"Sure. I'd love to have the company. Dad doesn't know who I am most of the time."

"Let me drive," Kyle said opening the door to his Jeep.

As they drove the five miles to the nursing home, they chatted about changes in the area like the new pier and the coffee shop that had recently been bought by some out-of-towner. Laughter filled the car, and Jenna longed for those old days where she could laugh and enjoy life with Kyle. Oh, how she wished things had turned out differently. How she wished Kaitlyn was his daughter and she was his wife.

They pulled into the Shady Grove nursing home, and Jenna's palms started to sweat. How would her father react to Kyle? Would he remember her? Him? She never knew what to expect when she visited him. It was heartbreaking to her that he barely remembered her name sometimes.

"Good morning, Mrs. Watson," a woman at the front desk said as they walked through the double glass doors. Kyle would never get used to hearing people call her that. She would never be "Mrs. Watson" in his mind. At the very least, she was Miss Davis, although he'd hoped years ago she would eventually be Mrs. Parker.

"Morning, Sue. How's Daddy today?"

"Confused, sweetie. We found him in Earl's room this morning."

"Oh, no. They didn't fight again, did they?"

"No, we caught him in time. He's over in the day room," she said as she answered the phone.

"Earl?" Kyle asked as they walked.

"Earl is Daddy's arch nemesis in here. They are constantly at odds, and Daddy ends up in his room a lot. He sometimes gets into Earl's chocolate stash, and that usually results in a very slow paced fist fight," Jenna said with a wry smile.

"Slow, but deadly?"

"Something like that," she said laughing as they entered the day room. Kyle was shocked at the sight of her father. Bill Davis was a tall, lanky man, and he'd always been strong. As a top basketball star in high school and college, he was always fit and trim, and he still was. His hair was no longer jet black, but solid white. The years had not been kind, as dementia had taken his facial expressions and mannerisms away.

Jenna crouched beside where he was sitting in a chair facing the window. "Hey, Daddy," she said kissing him on the cheek.

"Who are you?" he asked immediately. Her expression didn't change, which told Kyle that she was pretty used to that reception from her father.

"Daddy, you know who I am. It's your daughter, Jenna," she said smiling.

"Oh, that's right," he said gruffly.

"I brought an old friend today," she said waving Kyle over. He walked in front of the chair as the old man looked up at him. Bill's eyes widened.

"Kyle Parker," he said softly. Jenna's eyes widened too and then filled with tears.

"You remember me, Mr. Davis?" Kyle asked with a smile.

"How could I forget you? My daughter was obsessed with you. Did you know my daughter, Miss?" he asked Jenna.

"I sure did," she said, struggling to hold back the tears.

"Tell her to come see me sometime."

"How are you doing, Mr. Davis?" Kyle asked as he sat on the sofa next to the chair. Jenna turned and wiped away the stray tears that inevitably came when he didn't remember her.

"Oh, I'm fine. I'm getting out of here soon. I hurt my leg, so they have to do all their doctor stuff to fix it." Jenna shrugged at Kyle.

"How'd you hurt your leg?" Kyle asked playing along.

"Basketball, of course. Jump shot gone wrong," he said winking and smiling.

"I'm going to get your lunch ready, Daddy," Jenna said excusing herself.

"Is that your girlfriend?" Bill asked.

"No, sir. Just a friend."

"She's a pretty girl. You should ask her on a date," he said nodding his head. "Good women are hard to find."

"Yes, sir, they are."

"Listen, I'm glad I have you alone for a moment," Bill said leaning closer to Kyle.

"You are?"

"Yes. I've been meaning to tell you something, but I haven't seen you around town in a long time. You been on vacation?"

"Vacation? Yes, actually I just got back," Kyle said, still playing along with Bill's confused memory.

"Well, I need to say I'm sorry about something. See, my daughter, Jenna.... you know her?"

"I do."

"Well, she had a big crush on you, but her mother didn't like it. She didn't approve, and I went along with her. I shouldn't have done it. I knew how much you loved my daughter, but I didn't stick up for you or her. For that, I'm sorry."

Kyle sat there stunned as he processed what the man had just said to him. Jenna appeared beside her father with a tray of food.

"Hungry, Daddy?"

"I could eat a little something," he said chuckling as Jenna helped him up and walked him to the table. Kyle didn't move.

"You okay?" she whispered after she got her father settled.

"Huh? Oh, yeah..."

They sat with Bill as he ate, and he never said another word to Kyle. He didn't even seem to realize he was there at all. He focused on his food and the TV that sat off to the side of the table. The sadness in Jenna's eyes was palpable, and Kyle felt sorry for her.

"Daddy, I'm gonna go, okay?" Bill simply nodded without making eye contact. "He gets tired after he eats."

"It was nice to see you, Mr. Davis," Kyle said as he rubbed Bill's shoulder. Again, Bill just nodded and didn't look at him. It was obvious the moment of lucidity was gone.

When they reached Kyle's Jeep, Jenna waited for him to unlock the door. Instead, he walked around to her side of the vehicle and pulled her into his arms. Enveloped in her strawberry scent, he held her as tight as he'd ever held anyone. Her face pressed into his solid chest, she began to weep quietly. He let her cry and just pressed his mouth to the top of her head. They stood that way for several minutes before she pulled back a bit and looked at the wet mess she'd made on his shirt.

"I messed up your shirt," she said through a choked sob.

"No biggie. It can be washed."

"Thanks for that."

"For what?"

"For coming with me. For letting me cry all over you. For holding me. It's the safest I've felt in years," she admitted softly.

A knife went straight into Kyle's heart. The safest she'd felt in years. In his arms.

"I need to tell you something."

"What?"

"Your dad remembered me."

"I know. He said your name."

"No, I mean he remembered about you leaving me. He apologized. Said your mother pushed him to agree with her and that he was wrong. He said he knew how much we loved each other, and he should have stood up for us."

A huge smile crossed Jenna's face. "He remembered that?"

"Yep."

"Oh, Kyle, thank you! Thank you for telling me that!" she said hugging him tightly around the neck. Her shape, her form, her scent — it all felt so right in his arms. As warning bells went off in his head, he did his best to breathe in and out and avoid every manly urge he was having.

hen they arrived back at Kyle's house, Jenna finished unpacking a few things and then went to pick up Kaitlyn at school. As she drove back to her house, she thought about what her father had said to Kyle. For some reason, she finally had a small slice of peace about the situation.

Most people would have looked at their breakup as just a childhood rite of passage that everyone goes through, but not Jenna. Being with Kyle wasn't about being young or impetuous. She believed, and still did, that he was the one for her. He wasn't just some high school fling she had that came and went. He was a part of her soul, etched into the tiny crevices of her heart forever. That had been apparent during her marriage, and it still wasn't going away now. In fact, her feelings seemed to be increasing day by day.

"Go inside and get your room cleaned up," she

called to Kaitlyn as she bounded into the house. Jenna pulled the empty boxes from her car and started to take them into the house.

"Hey!" Becca called as she trotted across the yard.

"Hey there," Jenna said smiling from ear to ear.

"Ooohh... Something good must have put that smile on your face, girlfriend."

"Come sit a minute and I will fill you in on all the details," Jenna said throwing the boxes on the porch and sitting on the top step.

After a few minutes of intense girl gossip, Becca was up to date on the day's happenings.

"Wow. That is big news. I am thrilled about your Dad," she said patting Jenna's leg.

"Yeah, that was pretty amazing. Kyle always could cause some pretty amazing things to happen... " she said, with a big sigh and a lovesick look plastered across her face.

"Girl, you have it bad."

"What?"

"A case of the lovies," she said laughing as Jenna smacked her on the arm.

"I do not. I can't."

"Love wants what it wants, sweetie. Now is the right time to start putting the plan into action."

"You sound like a military commander," Jenna said rolling her eyes.

"Drop and give me twenty!"

"Very funny. I just don't know if this is the right

time to start making him jealous. Everything is so easy and good between us right now..."

"Is that what you want? A cordial relationship that's easy and good? Or do you want a sizzling hot rekindling of your passionate love affair?"

"Well, when you put it that way..."

"Good. It's settled. I'll call Frank tonight and we'll get the ball rolling."

"Exactly what are we doing?"

"Frank will have it covered. You just answer the call," she said rubbing her hands together.

"You should've been a secret agent."

"There's still time..."

The two women parted ways while Jenna went into the house to pack and cook dinner. The next couple of days were filled with packing, and she didn't really see Kyle. He seemed to be busy working, and she was glad to get a little distance. Their emotional connection had always been strong, and time had done nothing to lessen that.

The most unique part of their relationship had been the one that Jenna never told anyone. When she met Kyle, she was a virgin, and when she broke up with Kyle she was still a virgin. As hard as it was for most people to believe, she'd made a decision very young to stay "pure" until marriage. Kyle, a red blooded American male by every account, had respected her in that. They came close to breaking that pact a few times, but he'd always stopped himself.

Once she asked him why he was agreeing to wait for her to be ready and he'd said, "Don't you know, Jenna? The best things in life are worth waiting for and you're the best thing in my life." She'd almost jumped on him then.

She swore that part of the hurt in his eyes when she'd left was knowing the fact that some other man would have her in his bed. That he'd waited for nothing. It made her sick to her stomach that she'd given herself to Nick, although Kaitlyn had been the one good thing that came from that.

Nick didn't wait for her. But she didn't like to talk about that.

TODAY WAS the day Kyle had been waiting for. Jenna and Kaitlyn were officially moving in. Thankfully, they were out on break, so Kaitlyn could make a clean transition to her new school after a week-long vacation from school.

Most of their boxes had been transported to his house, and amazingly they had unpacked the majority of them. His cleaning and rehab crews were going to assess the old house tomorrow.

"Welcome home," Kyle said to Jenna and Kaitlyn as they walked into the house. The little girl hadn't seen it before, and she was mesmerized by all of the glass windows looking out over the beach.

"Can I walk outside?" she asked, pressing her hands together and grinning.

"Sure. Just don't get in the water," Jenna said. She and Kyle stood on the deck and watched as Kaitlyn ran all over the beach picking up seashells.

"She's going to love it here," he said.

"Yeah. I just hope..."

"What?"

"That she isn't too devastated when we have to leave."

"Let's not think about that right now," he said, knocking his shoulder into hers. "One day at a time."

"Right. One day at a time," she said nodding.

"So, what would you like for dinner?"

"Hmmm... Whatcha got?"

"Well, I was thinking some steaks on the grill, baked potatoes, salad."

"Yum. That sounds delicious after a long day of moving."

"Great. I'll go start marinating the steaks. Why don't you and Kaitlyn get settled into your rooms?"

Jenna called Kaitlyn up and took her to their rooms. As usual, Kaitlyn was thrilled with her new digs and ran downstairs to tell Kyle all about it.

"Mr. Kyle! Mr. Kyle!" she yelled as she ran downstairs. It occurred to Kyle that he'd never heard a child's voice in his house before.

"Yes, ma'am?" he said, picking her up and placing her on the counter.

"I love my room!" she squealed. Jenna came downstairs behind her and smiled at him.

"What?" he asked.

"When did you find time to paint it pink?" she asked with her hands on her hips.

"Yesterday," he admitted. "Surprise."

"It is so pretty! I can't believe how far I can see out my window. When will Snickers come by?"

"Tomorrow. Usually around seven in the morning, so you have to be ready."

"Got it! I'll go set my alarm," she said as she jumped down and ran back upstairs.

"Wow, she's mighty excited," he said laughing as he went back to preparing the baked potatoes.

"Can I help with something?"

"Well, if I remember correctly, you make a mean pitcher of sweet tea, don't you?"

"You remember well."

"Hard to forget."

The words slipped out before he could stop them, and he knew he had to stop doing that. He couldn't lead her to believe they had a future when they didn't.

"Is that your phone ringing?" he asked a moment later as she was pulling tea bags out of the box.

"I think it is," she said as she scurried to her purse and dug her phone from the bottom.

"Hello? Oh, hi, Frank! So nice to hear from you again! Lunch tomorrow? Sure, it's a date. How about noon? Great, I'll be ready."

"Big plans tomorrow?"

"First date," she mumbled as she tried not to make eye contact. Becca's idea was in full swing, but she was having a hard time keeping a straight face.

"Ah, I see. Good luck," he said all the while feeling like a dagger was jabbing through his skull. "And Kaitlyn?"

"Oh, I can take her to stay with Becca in the morning."

"Nah. No need. I'll be glad to keep her. I was planning to take her kite flying on the beach tomorrow anyway."

"Great. I just don't want you to ever feel like I'm using you as a babysitter or anything..."

"I can't always keep her, of course, but when I can I don't mind. She's a great kid."

"That she is," Jenna said as she poured hot water from the microwave over the tea bags. "So, do you date much these days?"

The tension floating through the air could have been cut with one of his dullest kitchen knives.

"Not lately, but I have dated in the past, of course."

"Of course. Anyone special?" she asked, nonchalantly.

"Do we really want to go there, Jenna?"

"I'd just like to know you were okay, Kyle."

"What does that mean?"

"That you were okay without me."

"I was never okay without you," he said, without thinking as he rolled the potatoes in aluminum foil. "I mean..."

"What?" she asked as she slid closer to him and turned to look at his face.

"I don't know what I mean. Can we just stop talking about all of this? It's in the past, for God's sake!" he said, slamming the roll of foil on the counter and storming out onto the deck. Running his fingers through his dark hair, he wondered how a woman could be so incredibly tempting and aggravating at the same time.

"Kyle..." she said softly as she followed him outside.

"Please, just give me a moment okay?" he said without turning around.

"Okay. I'll just finish up the tea."

"No, wait." Why couldn't he make up his mind? He turned around, and Jenna stood there waiting for an answer. "This is hard."

"I know it is."

"I don't know how to act around you. One part of me wants to swoop you into my arms and kiss you like you've never been kissed before. The other part of me wants to pick you up and throw you into that ocean over there for leaving me."

"Which part will win?" she asked smiling slightly.

"Neither. The part in the middle, the tiny logical part of my mind, is saying to be your friend. That's what I'm trying desperately to do."

"And do you think we can do that? I mean really?" she asked quietly as she walked toward him.

"I don't know..." he started to say before Kaitlyn came running outside.

"I think I see a sailboat!" she yelled as she ran toward the water.

"Moment broken," he said with a nervous laugh. "Better get back to those potatoes."

As he walked inside, leaving Jenna to tend to Kaitlyn, he wished he could take a cold shower.

JENNA TOOK a deep breath and tried to calm down. She adored Kaitlyn, but right now she could ring her neck for interrupting their conversation. What was he about to say?

The moment was over, and Kaitlyn monopolized the next few hours as children normally did. They ate dinner, laughed at her silly jokes and had ice cream on the beach. By nine o'clock, Kaitlyn was fast asleep on the sofa.

"She's all tuckered out, huh?" Kyle said as he walked into the living room where Jenna was pinned under Kaitlyn's legs.

"Yes. She played hard today for sure."

"Let me carry her up."

"You don't have to do that... " she said, but Kyle had already scooped her up like a baby and started toward the stairs. Watching him walk her up to her room and tuck her into bed like he was her father almost brought Jenna to tears. How she had longed for a family with Kyle, and now he was tucking in another man's child. She should have been his.

They tiptoed out of the room and back downstairs.

"Care for some wine?" he asked. She was starting to feel like she was on an extended date.

"Sure. But you know you don't have to entertain me every night while I'm here. I don't want to interfere with whatever you'd normally be doing."

"Hmmm... Interfering with my nightly television watching and scratching myself?"

Jenna started laughing and almost dropped the glass of wine he'd handed her. "I forgot how funny you are, Kyle Parker."

"Let's sit outside. It's a beautiful night," he said as they walked onto the deck. Jenna took a seat in one of the lounge chairs as Kyle scooted his next to hers. They both stared out at the waves crashing to shore in the distance.

"Kyle, I need to say something. Get something off my chest."

"Uh oh. That doesn't sound good."

"It's been bothering me for years..."

"Okay, out with it."

"You know how I was when we dated..."

"How you were?"

"A virgin," she whispered as if someone was eavesdropping on their conversation.

"Yes, I vaguely remember that," he said with a sly grin.

"I need to apologize about that. You waited for me for five long years, and then I ran off with a guy who had no intentions of waiting. I feel like I gave something away that wasn't mine to give."

"What? Of course it was yours to give, Jenna. I wasn't entitled to your virginity."

"I think you deserved it, though. Nick didn't."

"Did you sleep with him before you got married?"

"Yes. About two weeks after I met him, actually."

"What?" Kyle asked with a hint of anger in his voice.

"It's not what you think, Kyle. I didn't want to."

"He forced you?"

"In a manner of speaking, yes. We were at a party at college, alcohol was involved. He knew I was waiting, and that I had waited the whole time I dated you. He only waited until I was too drunk to say no and then he took his chance."

"Oh, my God." Kyle stood up and gripped the deck railing. She could tell he was ready to snap it in half.

"It's okay."

"No, it's not okay! No one was supposed to treat you that way. You were like a prize to me, Jenna. A breakable, beautiful vase that was worth sitting on the shelf and staring at. You were worth the wait, and I would have waited an eternity for you if that was what it took. If that idiot was here right now... "

"Kyle, I still married him. I forgave him at the time, but looking back on it makes me sick every time I think about it. I felt guilty for making you wait."

"You didn't make me wait, Jenna. I chose to wait."

"The point I'm getting at is that the reason I asked you earlier tonight if you had been okay after we broke up is that I've often wondered if another woman... "

"Fulfilled my needs, you mean?"

"Well, in a manner of speaking, yes."

"What do you hope the answer is, Jenna?"

"I'm not sure. On the one hand, I kind of wish that you never wanted another woman and pined for me, but I know that's not realistic. On the other hand, I've prayed all these years that you would be happy. And I know a person, a man especially, needs that physical part of a relationship. I guess I was just asking whether you've been fulfilled all these years because I would never want you to be lonely... " she trailed off. Kyle smiled at her.

"I don't think you really want to know the answer

to this question, Jenna. You're treading on dangerous waters here."

"I definitely don't want details," she said shaking her head. "I just want to know you've been okay."

"I've been okay."

"Good."

"Just okay, though, and that will never be good enough."

"What do you mean?"

"Like I told you before, there was no one good enough before you and there hasn't been anyone good enough after you. No one could ever measure up to the Jenna standard," he said waving his hand in front of her.

"Then why won't you consider..."

"Getting back together? No way. Can't do it. As much as all of my male testosterone might want that, I just can't put myself through it all again," he said standing up and leaning against the railing facing the ocean. She stood to meet him.

"How long are you going to do this?"

"Do what?"

"Put this wall up?"

"I have to."

"No, you don't," she said touching his arm. "It's me."

"That's why the wall is up, because it's you."

"I know, but give me a chance, Kyle."

He turned and looked at her with a heat in his

eyes that couldn't be tamed. It sent shivers up her spine, but before she could think much more, his mouth was covering hers. The warmth of his full lips brought back memories of a time long ago when she felt enveloped in his love every moment of every day. It was real, it was young and it was a lasting love that many people never get to feel.

She'd kissed him hundreds of times, but this was like the first time on that rock just a few feet away. She pulled his mouth closer to hers, interlacing her fingers behind his head. Suddenly, he pulled back and stepped a few feet away trying to catch his breath.

"What's wrong?" she said taking a step closer. He held up his hand.

"I said I couldn't do that." He looked up at the dark sky.

"But you did. Didn't you enjoy it?"

"More than you will ever understand, but it can't happen again. I'll never get that image out of my mind of you leaving me for another man, Jenna. I know it was a long time ago, but to me it was yesterday. When I used to look into your eyes, I saw this never-ending love but now I see someone who abandoned me and didn't want me as much as she thought she did."

"That's not true!" she argued. Again, he held up his hand.

"It's okay, Jenna. I'm not trying to start an argument or make you feel bad. I just want you to understand. That was a momentary mistake on my part, and it won't happen again." With that, he picked up the empty wine glasses and walked back into the kitchen.

She walked in behind him and finally spoke before going upstairs to bed. "Kyle, I need to correct one thing," she said softly. "I've always wanted you, and I always will. I think if you really studied these eyes of mine, you might just see that."

CHAPTER 10

*J*enna opened the door to her bedroom and closed it quietly behind her. That moment with Kyle had told her one thing for sure — he still loved her and she still loved him. That was all she needed to know.

Locking her door, she ran across the room and grabbed her cell phone. She quickly dialed Becca's number only to realize how late it was.

"Hello?" she said groggily.

"Oh, crap, sorry it's so late."

"Who is this?"

"Jenna, silly. Listen, I need some help."

"What's wrong?" Becca said, suddenly very alert and worried.

"I'm okay, it's nothing like that." Jenna recapped the evening's events for Becca, feeling like she was back in high school gushing about a crush.

"You're right. You need help."

Jenna chuckled to herself. She wasn't the most conniving person in the world, so it was hard for her to think about using a plan to get Kyle back. But one kiss was enough to tell her just how important it was for her to make things work between them again.

"Then help me," Jenna pleaded to her friend. Over the next few minutes, they came up with a plan that would be set into motion the next morning. Jenna crossed her fingers that it would work.

As the sun rose the next morning, Jenna opened her eyes and felt the warmth of a new day streaming through her window. If there was one thing she loved about the beach, it was the fact that every wave brought new life to her doorstep. She slipped on her robe and opened the doors to her deck as she took a seat outside. It was Saturday morning, which meant that Kaitlyn should still be fast asleep in her bed.

Instead, she saw something that took her breath away. Kyle was running down the beach holding Kaitlyn in his arms and swinging her around. She was cackling and laughing like Jenna had never heard before. The overwhelming sense of happiness that was bursting forth from her child caused tears to fill her eyes and anguish to crush her soul. How could Nick have abandoned her like he did? What kind of father did that?

Of course, she knew that getting a woman pregnant didn't make him a daddy. Kyle was daddy material. He was made to be a father, and she'd taken away the chance for him to be a father to her kids when she'd made such a silly, young mistake. She grieved over the thought that he might never forgive her, come back to her.

As she watched them crouched on her balcony, she steeled herself for the plan that Becca had come up with. Would it work? Or would it make things worse?

A part of her said to leave it all alone, be glad that he was back in her life as a friend and leave it at that. Another part of her knew that friendship with Kyle Parker would never be enough for her. He had carved away a piece of her heart all those years ago that she couldn't give to anyone else. Her failed marriage had been evidence of that fact.

She stood up for a moment to fix her robe and noticed Kyle staring at her from the beach. Kaitlyn was running around picking up shells again, but Kyle was motionless staring at her. What was he thinking? Slowly, a smile crept across his face and he held up a hand to wave at her. Then, he called Kaitlyn to walk back to the house. Jenna met them both downstairs.

"Mommy!"

"Good morning, sunshine! You're sure up early today."

"Kyle took me to the beach to see the sun come up. It was so cool!"

"That was a very sweet thing to do," Jenna said to Kaitlyn while looking at Kyle. He shrugged as he poured a cup of coffee. "Kaitlyn, why don't you run upstairs and take a shower? Miss Becca is coming to pick you up to spend the night with Lila."

"Yay!" Kaitlyn squealed as she ran up the stairs.

"Oh," Kyle said.

"What?"

"Nothing. It's just that I didn't know she was going to be gone this weekend. I bought a kite. I thought we agreed I'd keep her today."

She steeled herself for the conversation she was about to have. Hoping her experience in the high school drama production of Macbeth would somehow help her now, she began.

"Well, Kyle, I really appreciate that but we're not a family or anything. You're really just our landlord now, and I can't expect you to take up time with my daughter." He looked stunned.

"Are you saying you don't want me spending time with Kaitlyn anymore?"

"Of course not. That's up to you. I'm just saying I don't expect it. I mean, you aren't her father." At that point, she was worried she'd gone too far.

Kyle contorted his face into something that

resembled an angry smile mixed with definite smirking, and turned to refresh his coffee. He said nothing. After a moment, he turned around.

"Point made, Jenna," he said and walked out of the kitchen. What had she done?

As she walked back upstairs to get ready for the second part of her plan, she wondered if she was making the right decision.

KYLE PACED AROUND his bedroom wishing for something to punch. How could she talk to him that way? He knew Kaitlyn wasn't his real daughter, but he was already growing closer to her. He'd thought he was doing a good thing by spending time with her since her sack of crap father sure wasn't.

It was official. He'd never understand women.

Just as he walked out of his room, he heard Jenna's cell phone ring. She was talking to her date, who was on his way to pick her up soon. Kyle thought maybe he should leave until they were gone, but his curiosity was far too strong for that.

Acting as though nothing had happened, he walked back downstairs to find Kaitlyn sitting on the sofa with her bags packed.

"Whatcha doin', kiddo?"

"Waiting for Miss Becca."

"You like her?"

"Yeah. She's nice. And Lila is my BFF."

"BFF?"

"Best Friend Forever. Duh," Kaitlyn said rolling her eyes like she was ten years older than she was.

"Sorry, I'm not familiar with your groovy lingo," he said, tousling her hair.

"What does groovy mean?" she asked furrowing her eyebrows in a way that reminded him of Jenna when she was younger.

"Never mind. Well, when you get back, I bought you the coolest kite ever. We'll fly it out on the beach one day soon."

"Okay!" she yelped throwing her arms around his neck. The sudden display of affection took him off guard as he hugged her tightly. Even though she wasn't his child, he was already falling in love with her a little each day.

Just then, Jenna appeared on the stairs. Kyle quickly pulled away from the little girl. "Have a good time, sweetheart. See ya when you get back," he said as he walked into the kitchen.

A few minutes later, Becca came by and picked Kaitlyn up. It was 11:45, and Kyle knew that Jenna's date would be there very soon.

"I'm going to be leaving in a few minutes," Jenna said resting her elbows on the breakfast bar.

"Okay. Have fun," he said, as if he could care less. In reality, it was eating him up inside. He'd already watched her leave with another man once in his life, and he certainly didn't want to do it again. But this guy was a stranger to her, and he wasn't going to leave her alone in the house with a stranger picking her up.

"Kyle..." she started to say, but the doorbell rang and interrupted her thought.

"I'll get that," she said as she trotted to the front door. In her pink sundress and silver strappy sandals, she looked beautiful as usual. "Hi, Frank! Oh, roses, they're lovely. Thank you! Let me just put them in water." He could hear a man's voice and then footsteps coming toward the kitchen. A GQ-looking blond haired guy appeared behind her, smiling brightly.

"Hi. Frank Gibson," he said holding out his hand to Kyle.

Kyle stared at him for a moment, smiled and then held out his hand. "Nice to meet you, Frank."

"Well, I guess we'd better get going," Jenna said after putting the flowers into water. "See ya later, Kyle." She took Frank's arm and out the door they went, leaving Kyle standing in his kitchen shaking his head.

FRANK WAS A NICE GUY, and Jenna didn't mind hanging out with him, but she would much rather have been at home with Kyle. Even sitting on the beach with him or watching him drink his morning coffee was enough to keep Jenna entertained. After so many years without him in her life, she was happy to have him around again. His spirit lit up every room and made her days worth living again. As a mother, Kaitlyn did that for her too, but as a woman she'd been pretty dead inside for many years.

"Jenna?" Frank said waving his hand in front of her face.

"Oh, sorry," she said. "I was somewhere else." She took the last bite of her sandwich and looked out at the ocean. Frank had brought her to a small beach-front restaurant for their lunch date.

"I bet I know where," he said laughing as he took one of her French fries.

"I bet you do. Why do men have to be so difficult?"

"Girl, who knows? I've been trying to figure that out for years," he said waving his hand in the air. Frank was most-decidedly gay, but he was more than willing to help Jenna with her plan. Becca had been friends with him for many years, and they'd acted in many drama productions around the Southeast together. As a part-time actor, he relished the opportunity to play Jenna's new suitor.

"He didn't even look like he cared when you came to pick me up. I was hoping for a much stronger reaction..."

"Then maybe we need to crank it up a notch," Frank said with a glint in his eyes.

"How so?"

"Well, I have a few ideas," he said rubbing his hands together. For the next few minutes, he went over his ideas with Jenna, and her eyes bugged out of her head.

"Seriously? You think that will work?"

"Well, if it doesn't then I would say he's a lost cause, girl."

"True. Alright, let's do it. Let's go for broke tonight," she said, shaking his hand across the table.

KYLE WALKED around the craft store trying to figure out what Jenna would need. She had loved painting since he'd known her, and her talent was amazing. He never understood why her parents didn't see it.

No matter what, she was his friend and he wanted to do something nice for her. He thought at the very least, Kaitlyn deserved to see her mother doing something she loved. It occurred to him that the little girl had probably never seen her mother paint.

He gathered up the paint, brushes, easel and other supplies he'd bought and drove home. When he pulled into the driveway, there was a car there that he didn't recognize. A man stepped out of it dressed in what he referred to as "city clothes." It was obvious this man wasn't living in their more laid-back beach area.

"Can I help you?" Kyle asked as he got out of the car carrying a bag of paints.

"I'm looking for Jenna Watson," he said gruffly.

"Who are you?" Kyle asked equally as gruffly.

"That's really none of your business."

"Well, as I own the property you're currently standing on, I'd say it is my business."

The man huffed under his breath. "My name is Nick Watson, and I've come to see my daughter."

Kyle balled his fists down by his side and struggled to keep his emotions under control. The last thing he needed to do was attack this idiot and end up in jail over it.

"What in the hell are you doing here?"

"I see you know my name," he said with a smirk. "And I already told you I'm here to see my daughter, so where is she?"

"She's not here."

"Where is she?" he asked angrily.

"None of your business," Kyle said as he passed Nick and unlocked the front door.

Nick pushed past him and started yelling throughout the house. "Kaitlyn! Kaitlyn!"

"I told you she's not here," Kyle said putting down the bag. Nick glanced at it and saw the paints.

"Where is Jenna?"

"She's out."

"Out where?"

"Look, I have nothing to say to you, man. You need to leave before I call the police."

"She can't keep my child from me," Nick said through gritted teeth.

"Are you kidding me? You're the one who disappeared from that little girl's life and then let the only home she's ever known get foreclosed."

"Foreclosed?"

"Yes, foreclosed. Your child was going to be on the streets if I didn't step in."

"This is all Jenna's fault!"

"How is that? Aren't you the one who wrecked your marriage by sleeping with a nurse at the hospital where you work?" Nick's eyes got big.

"She told you that?" he asked indignantly.

"Yes, among other things."

"Who are you anyway? Her new fling?" Something about the way he said it enraged Kyle. He knew better than anyone just how pure Jenna had been when he married her. How could he act like she was some kind of tramp?

"Watch your mouth. I'm warning you," Kyle said. Nick's eyes suddenly shifted to a plaque hanging on the wall by the fireplace. It was one of Kyle's "Million Dollar Producer" plaques from when he sold real estate under his mother's company.

"Oh, my God. Kyle Parker? You're the infamous

Kyle Parker? Boy, she didn't waste any time..." he said with a snide grin.

"Not that it is any of your business, but we're just friends."

"Right. You're telling me that she spent our marriage pining for you and being in love with you, but now you're only her friend? I'm sure you've already been in her pants a few times by now... "

Before Kyle could think, his fist was connecting with Nick's right eye. Nick fell backward and landed in a chair in the living room. As blood trickled down his face, he jumped up and charged at Kyle. Kyle pushed him again sending him cascading to the floor. One thing was certain — this guy was a wuss.

"You're going to jail," Nick yelled from the floor.

"Really? Good. Call the police. While we're at it, I'll remind them that you haven't paid your child support in months so they can take you to prison right away." Nick glared at him as he stood up slowly.

Before the men could continue, the front door opened. Jenna was wrapped in Frank's arms kissing him passionately. He carried her inside and shut the door with his foot.

"Oh, Frank... " she purred in a seductive voice. "Stay with me tonight... "

"Of course, baby... " he said back.

Suddenly, her eyes cut over to the scene in the

living room with Nick's face bleeding and Kyle towering over him. She jumped from Frank's arms.

"Oh, my God! What's going on here?" she asked. Frank stayed at the front door before slowly walking into the living room.

"Well, there she is... " Nick said. "Wow, you work fast. Got one man letting you live in his house and another one about to sleep with you. Nice, Jenna."

"You want some more?" Kyle asked raring back his fist. Jenna ran over and pulled on his arm.

"Kyle, don't. He's not worth it," she said as he slowly lowered his arm.

"Nick, why are you here?"

"I want my daughter."

"She's not here, and you haven't bothered to contact her in months."

"I've been very busy." He wiped a trickle of blood from his mouth.

"Too busy to pay your child support?"

"After the way you ruined our marriage, I'm not paying one dime that goes to you."

"It doesn't go to me. It goes to your daughter. I lost the house because of you, Nick. Your daughter's whole life has been uprooted because you're holding a grudge against me. You slept with another woman, for goodness sake!"

"And you know why," he sneered at her. "Apparently, your friend Kyle doesn't."

Kyle shot a confused glance at Jenna, but she was

far too preoccupied with getting Nick out of the house.

"Look, you know I would never keep Kaitlyn from you, but you have to go through the proper channels. You can't just show up here and demand to see her. If she'd been here, this would have scared her to death. Think about your child for once, Nick! Stop thinking about yourself. Have your attorney contact my attorney if you want to work out a visitation arrangement, but stay away from this house!"

"Poor Kyle. I guess he wasn't able to get you back since you seem to have already moved on with this loser," he said pointing at Frank.

Kyle suddenly laughed, which seemed completely inappropriate to everyone around him. "Get out, you moron."

Nick turned and walked to the front door, but before he left he turned back around and directed his attention to Jenna.

"You should be honest with people, Jenna. Our marriage was over long before I slept with that nurse and you know it. Quit playing the victim. Every bit of this is your fault, and one day Kaitlyn will see that, too. Our daughter is going to hate you for breaking up our family," he said before walking out and slamming the front door.

Jenna stood in the foyer; her shoulders slumped as if the weight of the world was on them. Sobs started to break free, and Frank ran to her and put his arm around her. Kyle walked up behind them.

"Listen, you two, this has to stop. I know what you're doing. Jenna, were you going to sleep with him to prove your point?"

"What?" she asked turning around with her eyes already puffy and red.

"Frank is gay, and you know it. Using him to make me jealous is a pretty juvenile thing to try, don't you think?" Frank avoided eye contact and Jenna stomped her foot.

"How did you know?"

"Because he once dated a friend of mine. Caleb Green?"

Frank smiled. "Oh, yes, hunky Caleb Green. Fire-fighter. Hot." Kyle laughed.

"Yes, he's a firefighter. Hot? I wouldn't know," he said.

"I'm so embarrassed," Jenna said putting her hand over her face. "Frank, can you leave us now?" she asked. He nodded and gave her a quick hug before bolting out the front door.

"Jenna?" Kyle said, ducking down and trying to see her face.

"I can't look at you."

Kyle pried her hands away from her face and pushed her chin up with his fingers. "Look at me."

Slowly, she raised her eyes to meet his. His

insides tightened up every time he looked into her big green eyes.

"Jenna, what were you trying to accomplish by going out with a gay guy, exactly?"

"Do we have to talk about this?" she begged.

"Yes, we do."

"Fine. I wanted to make you jealous. I wanted you to seethe with jealousy until you couldn't stand it. I wanted you to forgive me and let me back into your heart!" she said throwing her hands in the air.

"I forgave you a long time ago, and you've always been in my heart."

"Kyle, when you say stuff like that it makes my heart hurt. I feel like you're right here in front of me, yet you're a million miles away. I can't just pretend I don't love you. I thought living here would be easy, but it's only been a couple of days and I can't stand it anymore," she said walking into the living room and plopping down on the sofa.

"I know. It's been a lot harder for me, too. Maybe we need to take a break from talking about this for a little bit. There's something I need to do. Why don't you go take a long, hot bath or go sit down by the beach for awhile. Calm down from Nick's visit."

"You want me to leave you alone for awhile?" she asked confused.

"Yes. I need a little space for a few minutes. Maybe half an hour. Can you give me that?" She nodded slowly and walked out the back door and down to the beach.

WHAT WAS he thinking right now? He'd sent her away after she'd just admitted how much she still loved him. Maybe he was looking for a nice way to let her down easy. Maybe he was calling a hotel for her to stay in. Relaxing on the beach didn't work when she couldn't relax.

She watched the waves rolling in and out and tried to slow her breathing down. She had always been far too spastic to meditate, but she wished that she could.

"Jenna!" Kyle's voice called from behind her. He was up on the deck waving her back to the house. It had only been twenty minutes, but maybe he wanted to get this ugliness over with.

She walked hesitantly up the stairs praying for a miracle. Maybe he had called Pastor Henry and wanted to marry her on the spot. Yeah, in her dreams.

"Everything okay?" she asked when she saw him standing in the living room with a big grin on his face. Certainly not the reception she expected.

"We'll see what you think in a minute," he said as he pointed at the stairs and ushered her to follow him.

CHAPTER 11

*A*s she followed him up the stairs, she worried what he had up his sleeve. He seemed awfully happy for someone who might be throwing her out of the house at any moment.

"Okay, close your eyes," Kyle said as he grabbed her arm to lead her where he wanted her to go. Jenna closed her eyes and allowed him to guide her around the corner into the room he used for his home office. "Open your eyes."

As she opened her eyes, she was completely stunned. Gone were his desk and computer, and in their places were an easel, paints, blank canvases and other art supplies. The drapes were open overlooking the ocean, and there was a brand new coffee maker on the dresser.

"What is this?" she said softly with her hand over her heart.

"It's your art studio," he said with a soft smile that she wanted to kiss. Jenna walked around, lightly touching everything he'd bought for her.

"I don't understand. Why did you do this for me, Kyle?" she asked, turning around and looking at him.

"Because you need this, Jenna. Do you know the most painful part of seeing you again? It was seeing that the old Jenna was missing. Your very soul depends on your love of painting, and someone took that away from you along the way. I just wanted to give it back because I want Kaitlyn to know who her real mother is."

She could hardly breathe as she listened to his words. A stray tear rolled down her cheek and she quickly brushed it away.

"I hope this is okay with you... " he said, as if he was worried he'd upset her.

"Oh, Kyle, of course it's okay with me. It's more than okay. No one else on Earth would have done this for me but you. It's like you've always been able to see straight into my very soul, and I wish to God I could explain how much I wish I could go back and change things... "

"This isn't about that, Jenna. This is just about me wanting to see the old Jenna again. Maybe it's a little selfish, but I miss her. I used to love to see that light in your eyes when you'd finished a painting. In fact, stay here for a second," he said as he walked out of the room.

Jenna walked to the easel and ran her fingers across the blank canvas he had placed there. She always looked at those blank canvases as dreams waiting to happen. She wanted to paint something on it that would give hope and inspiration to the person who owned it.

"Look," Kyle said from behind her. She turned around to see a painting she had completed in her senior year of high school. It was an ocean scene and featured their rock in the middle.

"You kept it," she said, walking over and touching it.

"It's one of my most prized possessions. Of course I kept it."

"Even after what I did to you?" she asked, looking amazed.

"Jenna, I was never really angry with you. I was hurt, disappointed, devastated..."

"Okay, okay. I already feel bad enough!" she said, jokingly punching him in the arm. "What about your office? Your business is way more important than my hobby."

"I have a laptop I work from most of the time. I can set up on the deck or my bedroom. And painting isn't your hobby, Jenna. You and I both know that."

"I don't know how I will ever thank you, Kyle. It's hard to believe how incredibly hopeless I was just a short time ago, and you've helped me turn everything around. Thank you so much," she said as she reached around his chest and hugged him tightly. He hesitated for a second, but eventually wrapped his arms around her and pressed his mouth against the top of her head. "I know this can't ever happen between us, Kyle, but please know how much I regret my choice. Kaitlyn should have been your daughter, and we should've been a family." She felt him start to tense up, so she eased out of the embrace.

"Are you excited about starting your new job on Monday?" he asked as he backed away from her.

"Oh, of course. I love your mother."

"She's pretty excited to have you there."

"Good."

The uneasiness in the room was apparent, and Jenna knew she had to start talking about Nick.

"I'm sorry Nick showed up here," she said as she sat down on the floor. He followed her lead and sat across from her.

"He's a jerk." Typical Kyle — getting right to the point.

"Yes, he is."

"What did you ever see in that idiot?"

"Well, at first he was a nice guy. He helped me find my way around college, he was polite, and he complimented me. Then, once I broke things off with you, he started to change a bit. By the time we were married, I'd already realized the huge mistake I had made but I couldn't face it. I just couldn't."

"Did he ever abuse you?" Kyle asked with a steely glaze in his eyes.

"Kyle, I don't want to talk about this... " she said, putting her face in her hands.

"Oh, my God. He hit you?"

"A few times, yes."

Kyle stood up and started pacing the room. He was running his fingers through his hair and breathing in and out deeply.

"Jenna, why didn't you get help?"

"Because it wasn't everyday, and he had this amazing way of making me think it was my fault. I did tell my mother once."

"And what did she say?" Kyle asked already knowing the answer.

"She said that Nick was going to be a rich doctor one day and that if I held on long enough, at least I could get a lot of alimony when we divorced."

Kyle fumed. "I'm so sorry, Jenna. I cannot believe your mother."

"Yeah, me either. But I could've left, and I didn't. And then I did some things that made Nick into even more of a monster."

"What things?"

"I can't really talk about it, but let's just say that Nick believes I caused him to cheat."

"That makes no sense, Jenna."

"I can't tell you, Kyle. It's just too embarrassing. And you'll think I am a horrible, disloyal person. You already think you can't trust me, and this won't help matters any."

"Jenna, you should know by now that you can tell me anything."

"Not this, Kyle. I just can't," she said as she stood up and walked to her bedroom, shutting the door behind her.

As KYLE DROVE his car toward Jenna's old house, he thought about everything she'd said and everything Nick had said, too. It was all so confusing. What was it that Jenna had done that made her think the divorce was her fault? It just didn't make sense, and why couldn't she tell him?

He pulled into the driveway just as evening fell, so he took some time to sit on the front porch and watch the sun turn to shades of pink over the ocean. He needed to check a few things in the house, but mostly he needed some time away from Jenna.

"Can I help you?" a woman said as she crossed from her yard to his.

"I own this house," he said a little too sharply. She stopped in her tracks and then smirked a bit more than he would've liked.

"Kyle Parker, I assume?"

"Oh, you must be Jenna's friend. Becca, right?"

"That's me."

"How are Lila and Kaitlyn doing?" he asked with a smile.

"Fine."

"I'm sorry, did I do something to irritate you?" he asked, furrowing his eyebrows.

"As a matter of fact, yes you did. You hurt my best friend, and I don't take too kindly to that."

"Jenna?"

"Of course. Wow, you are a perceptive one, aren't you?"

"And you're a spitfire, aren't you?"

"I take that as a compliment," she said as she pulled a dead rose bud off Jenna's bush.

"Okay, so what did I do that was so terrible? Foreclose? Because I had no idea this was Jenna's house." He walked closer to her and crossed his arms.

"No, that's old news. I'm talking about the fact that she has ached for you for so long, and you move her in and then tell her there is no chance for you two. That sounds pretty mean to me," she said crossing her arms to match his.

"Seriously? You just met me. You weren't even around when we dated. You have no idea... "

"Trust me, I know a lot more than you think. Probably more than you even know." It suddenly dawned on him that she knew the secret. Jenna had told her, but why not him?

"Mind if I come in for a bit?" he asked pointing at her house instead of his.

"You want to come in my house?" she asked cocking her head.

"Yeah. Just for a minute. I need to ask you something."

"Ask me on my porch," she said pointedly as she turned and walked toward her house.

"Very neighborly of you," he said chuckling to himself.

As they crossed the yard, he could see Lila and Kaitlyn playing on the swing in the backyard. He was careful not to let them see him since he wanted this conversation to be uninterrupted.

"Before you start asking me questions, I'd like to ask you one. And please note that my BS detector has a low threshold for crap. So don't play with me, okay?"

"You're kind of scary," he said sitting back in a chair.

"Glad you think so. Anyway, please listen to my question and answer honestly. I promise it won't go further than this porch."

"Okay..."

"Do you still love Jenna?" she asked staring into his eyes.

"With every part of my heart." Becca's mouth hung open. She apparently wasn't expecting that answer.

"Then why? Why not return her love and live happily ever after?" she asked throwing her hands up.

"It's complicated."

"No it's not."

"You're a bossy one, Becca."

"Don't change the subject. Why can't you give your relationship another chance if you love her like that? Do you know how hard it is to find that kind of love?"

"I do. I've been trying for over a decade."

"Then what is holding you back?"

"Did Jenna tell you about our breakup?"

"Yes. I've heard all about it. How she saw you standing there and watched, as you got smaller in the rearview mirror and how she felt so bad and guilty... "

"Right. Well, from my perspective, she drove right out of my life for another man. That means she didn't love me as much as she loved him, and I can't trust that she wouldn't do that again at some point."

"That was so long ago. "

"It still hurts, Becca. You have no idea how close Jenna and I were. It was like God made us exactly for each other. When she left me for that jackass, I was wrecked for a long time. I can't do it again."

"Wow, I can't believe I'm about to do this."

"Do what?" he asked.

"Listen, Kyle, I am a good friend to Jenna. I've

held her confidences for so long, but sometimes you have to have priorities. And I would rather see her deliriously happy and have her mad at me than take a chance that you two won't end up together."

"You know the secret?"

"You know there's a secret?"

"I know Nick showed up at my house this morning spouting off a bunch of crap about how she ruined their marriage."

"Oh, God. Is she okay?"

"Yeah. She's okay. She was very shaken up."

"He's an abusive creep, Kyle. He has to stay away from her, you hear me?"

"Don't worry. He won't get past me ever again."

"I believe you. I don't know why, but I do. Okay, so there is a secret that Jenna won't tell you about her marriage, and I'm going to because I love her. I want her to get everything she's ever wanted, and that happens to be all wrapped up in this package you call Kyle," she said as she waved her hand in front of him.

"I'm dying here. Please, give me the scoop."

"Alright. Where do I begin? When Jenna married Nick, she did it to appease her mother and father. You know that. Then Nick started getting abusive, and she tried to get out but he threatened her several times."

"Jackass," Kyle muttered under his breath.

"Agreed. Anyway, she tried to stick it out because

she was getting a lot of pressure from her mother. Just as she was about to leave him anyway, she found out she was pregnant with Kaitlyn. She couldn't do it, Kyle," she said shaking her head.

"I get all that, but why is it a secret?"

"It's not. I'm getting to that. When they moved to this house, Nick was packing up boxes and he found one that he never expected. You see, Jenna never got over you, Kyle. She never stopped wanting you."

"What was in the box, Becca?" he asked, growing impatient.

"Dozens of letters that she'd written to you over the years including one written the night before her wedding. She never mailed any of the letters because she thought you hated her, but she kept each one to remind herself of you. Every letter talked about how she still loved you and not him and how she wished that she could find her way back to you. She knew she'd made a mistake, and those letters were just her catharsis. They were the therapy she couldn't get without Nick finding out. They were her only connection to you."

"Oh, my God... " he said softly.

"Then, the letters weren't enough anymore. She found out that you were working for your mother in January Cove, so she started driving through town occasionally. She'd spot you standing in the parking lot of the real estate office or down at the beach, and she'd sit in her car and cry. I even went with her once when Kaitlyn was a baby. Nick thought we were going shopping. I remember she picked up a newspaper in January Cove when you made Agent of the Year. She cut out that picture and it was in her box, too. She kept the box hidden behind her shoes in the top of her closet, and Nick never would've found it except Kaitlyn got sick the morning of the move and Jenna was preoccupied with her."

Kyle stood and ran his fingers through his hair as he stared out at the ocean. Becca stood up and touched his arm.

"Look, Kyle, I know this is hard to hear all at once, but Jenna never stopped loving you or wanting you. She knows it was wrong to love another man while she was married, but Nick kept threatening her if she left. Of course, once he found the box, he made her life miserable. He started cheating, abused her more and started drinking on top of everything else. Finally, he left her penniless and a single mother. Trust me, Kaitlyn is better off without him as her father, and it is for Kaitlyn that I tell you all of this. Jenna has told me how much she wishes Kaitlyn was your daughter."

"I do too," he admitted. "I feel like I've always been her daddy."

"Then fix this, Kyle. It's in your hands. I believe there is always a moment in time where everything that has gone wrong can be made right. This is that time."

Becca's words ricocheted around in his brain like a stray bullet. She was right. Jenna had never really left him. She'd continued to love him like he'd loved her.

"Where are the letters?"

"She asked me to hide them here so you'd never find them. She was afraid that you'd think less of her for longing for you even after she was married. Didn't make sense to me, but she was adamant."

"Can I have them?"

"Kyle, I don't know. Jenna's already going to be mad at me..."

"No, she won't. I promise. I just need to hold them in my hands and see them for myself. Please."

Becca stood there for a moment trying to make a decision. Finally, she sighed and pointed for him to go into the house. As he waited in the foyer, she went upstairs into the attic. Just then, Kaitlyn and Lila came running through the house.

"Kyle!" Kaitlyn yelled as she ran into his arms.

"Hey, sweetheart," he said picking her up. "Having fun?"

"Yes, tons of fun! But I'm ready to fly our kite!"

"Tomorrow, I promise, okay?" he said smiling. Becca walked back down the stairs and stopped to take in the scene.

"Okay! See ya tomorrow!" she said, as she skipped back out of the room with Lila.

Becca held out the brown cardboard box, and Kyle took it carefully.

"Thanks."

"Please don't hurt her, Kyle. Her heart is so fragile," Becca said in a serious tone.

"I know. I won't hurt her."

Becca rubbed his arm, smiled and walked out of the room. Kyle carried the box to his car and prepared to step back in time.

JENNA SAT on her bed looking out over the ocean and wondering how life went on when hers was in such turmoil. She loved him so much, yet it could never be. Her mind and her heart couldn't process that information.

When he'd left earlier, she knew it was because of her and that stupid secret she was keeping. She'd toyed with the idea of telling him, but what kind of woman would he think she was with that information? She was trying to prove her honesty and loyalty, and that story certainly wouldn't do it. She'd been emotionally unfaithful to her husband almost since day one, so didn't she deserve his adultery? Not the physical abuse, but she felt sure she deserved his cheating. He'd told her so many times.

Suddenly, she got a text from Becca. It simply said, "*Don't hate me.*" What on Earth did that mean?

Becca wouldn't answer, and Jenna had an uneasy feeling.

~

As Kyle sat on the pier under a light, he slowly opened the box. What he found shocked him. His football jersey, the ticket stub to their first movie date together, the small teddy bear he'd won at the fair for her. Then he saw the picture of himself from the newspaper and a stack of letters. There must have been at least 50 of them. He rubbed his fingers over the rubber band holding them together. Reading them would be one of the hardest things he'd ever done.

My dearest Kyle,

Today, I watched as you got smaller and smaller in my rearview mirror, and I wondered what in the world I was doing. I pray that you know how much I love you still. I guess you can call me a weak woman because I can't seem to go against my parents' wishes. I know that I will spend the rest of my life regretting choosing a man I don't love as much as I love you. Just please try to understand how sorry I am.

Love you forever,

Jenna

Kyle took a moment to catch his breath. It was so hard to look back now and comprehend just what a hold Jenna's parents had on her at the time. He opened another letter and then another. He read each one while holding his breath as it became more and more apparent that Jenna was abused by her husband such that she couldn't have left if she'd wanted to.

My dearest Kyle,

I wonder what you're doing right this very minute. I pray for your safety and happiness every night as I am going to sleep. I wonder if you have a special woman in your life who is holding you as she sleeps. While I want the best for you, it feels like someone is drilling through my heart to think of another woman enjoying what should be mine. I made a stupid mistake, Kyle, and I pay for it daily. But now I am a mommy to a beautiful one-year-old daughter, and my options in life are limited. I can't leave, but I can't stay. I don't know what to do anymore.

I love you,

Jenna

He could feel the torture in her soul as he read each letter and got a peek into what Jenna's life had been for all those years. One choice had taken her down a path that was never meant to be hers. She was supposed to have the best. He was supposed to have given it to her.

The final letter was written a little over a year ago.

My dearest Kyle,

This will be my final letter to you because I can't do it

anymore. Every time I write to you, my heart aches and my eyes swell with tears. My four year old caught me crying yesterday, and that is too hard to explain. I won't damage my daughter because of my silly mistakes. I hope that you are happy, Kyle. I miss you every day of my life, and I can only hope that you will one day forgive me for leaving you. Every ounce of me wants to load my baby into the car and find you, but I know that you would never accept me back into your life. And I don't blame you. This life I'm living with a man I don't love is the punishment I deserve for throwing you away like trash. I'm so incredibly sorry.

I will love you forever,

Jenna

His heart broke for her. He threw everything back in the box and ran for his car. She didn't need to suffer one moment longer.

CHAPTER 12

*K*yle couldn't get back to the house fast enough. He was pretty sure he ran at least one red light, but January Cove was slow-paced enough that it didn't matter much.

He pulled into the driveway and ran inside the house. "Jenna?" he called out to her as he walked up the stairs, but she wasn't there. For a moment, he feared that she'd left him after their conversation earlier, but then he heard the ocean. That had to mean a door or window was open somewhere in the house.

He ran back downstairs to see the back door open and blowing in the sea breeze. It was dark outside with only the moon glimmering off the waves. He tried to see, but he couldn't make out anything on the beach. She wasn't on the deck, so he kicked off his shoes and began walking toward the water.

"Jenna?" he called as he walked, and then he saw her. She was sitting up on their rock staring out at the waves as they crashed to shore. "Hey. Are you okay?" he asked softly as he walked up beside her. There was enough moonlight to tell that she'd been crying, and she held a glass of wine in her hand.

"I guess so," she said quietly without looking at him.

"Mind if I come up?" he asked. She nodded, still without making eye contact, and he climbed up on the rock beside her. It reminded him of all those times they'd sat on that rock, sometimes kissing for hours as they watched the waves come in and out. "We need to talk."

"First, I need to talk," she said stoically.

"Okay... "

"Kaitlyn and I are moving out."

"What?" he asked feeling like someone had punched him in the gut.

"It's for the best, Kyle. I can't do this. I thought I could, but maybe I was just holding onto the hope that we still had something. I can't put myself through torture every day. I did that during my marriage, for a different reason of course, but I swore I'd never live in a situation where I was miser-able. And I am miserable when I look at you. Every-thing in me says to hug you and kiss you and cuddle up next to you in bed at night, but I can't. I'll never have that chance again. I can't stay here, and I certainly cannot let my daughter get attached to a man that won't be in her life that long. I mean, how long will it be before some woman finally catches the elusive Kyle Parker?" she said with a bit of a slur to her words. How much wine had she consumed, he wondered.

"Jenna, you don't understand..."

"Yes I do understand. I hurt you, now you hurt me. That's how life works."

"You know that isn't true with us, Jenna. I would never hurt you for revenge or anything else."

"You don't know the things I've done. If you did, you wouldn't trust me either. I deserved Nick's cheating. Not the physical hitting, but I deserved the cheating."

"No you didn't, Jenna! Stop saying crap like that. How many glasses of this have you had?" he asked as he took the half empty glass from her hands.

"I stopped counting... " she said with a drunken giggle. At that moment, Kyle realized he couldn't tell her what he'd read yet. She was far too tipsy to understand, and he wanted her to be fully present when he told her.

"Come on, Jenna. Let's go back to the house," he said as he attempted to get her up.

"No."

"No?" Her argumentative side was coming back

out. He remembered it well. He jumped down off the rock and looked up at her.

"No."

"Look, Jenna, you're too tipsy to be out here alone. Now, come on."

"I said no. For goodness sakes, I'm a grown woman!" she shrieked loud enough that he was sure the neighbors could hear.

"That's it. I've had enough of this," he said as he grabbed her around the waist and threw her over his shoulder. As anticipated, she started kicking her legs and flailing her arms, hitting him squarely in the back between his shoulder blades. The more pain she inflicted, the faster he walked, trying desperately to get her into the house before someone called 911 and accused him of abusing or abducting a woman.

When he finally reached the back door, he tossed her on the sofa and went back to lock the door.

"You can be such a jerk!" she yelled as she stood up and stomped her foot on the floor. He struggled not to laugh, but she had always reminded him of a three-year-old when she got too tipsy. It seemed to bring out the immature, flamboyant, incredibly honest side of Jenna. She was so petite that it didn't take much alcohol to do her in, and he was fairly certain she didn't drink very often given her current state.

Kyle ignored her temper tantrum and started a

pot of coffee. He knew it was going to be a long night.

THE CLOCK SAID THREE AM. How long had she been asleep? The last thing she remembered was beating on Kyle's back as he carried her into the house, although she couldn't remember exactly why she was so mad at him. Her head was pounding. Why was she such a lightweight when it came to alcohol?

She sat up in her bed and realized she was still wearing her Capri pants and t-shirt she'd worn to the beach. Why hadn't she changed into her pajamas? A wave of nausea rolled over her as she turned on the bedside lamp.

"You okay?" Kyle said from a chair in the corner.

"Kyle! You scared the crap out of me! What are you doing over there?" she asked with her hand resting over her pounding heart.

"Care for a glass of wine?"

"Very funny. Seriously, what are you doing in here?"

"I was afraid you'd run off again, and honestly I don't think my shoulder blades can take the abuse." He stood up and walked to the bed, sitting down beside her.

"I'm sorry I hurt you. Again."

"Jenna, are you sober enough to have a very serious conversation now?"

"Is that why you were looking for me earlier? To have another serious conversation? Because I can't take it anymore, Kyle. I was serious about moving out. I do remember saying that."

"Can you just listen for a minute?" She shrugged and nodded her head as she sat back against the headboard for support. He turned and faced her. "Jenna, I know."

"Know what?"

"About the letters." She looked at him for a moment before shaking her head.

"How can you know? That's impossible. Wait... Becca? She told you?" Remembering the cryptic text message she'd received, Jenna finally put it together.

"Don't be mad at her."

"I'm going to kill her!" Jenna said running her fingers through her hair. "How could she break a confidence like that?"

"Because she loves you, and she wants to see you happy."

"My God, what must you think of me now? You already thought I was disloyal when I left you for Nick... "

"Jenna, I don't think any less of you because of this. In fact, if it's even possible, I think more of you."

"You think more of me when I wasn't totally committed to my marriage?"

"You were committed, but you were always being pulled back here, to me. We had something that most people would kill for, and your parents convinced you it wasn't real."

"But I should have been stronger than that, Kyle."

"You were young, Jenna. Would you leave me now if your parents told you to?"

She thought for a moment. "Never in a million years."

"When we're young, everything our parents say is the law. Your parents were particularly critical and had raised you to think that their way was the only way."

"But surely you knew all this before, Kyle, so what has changed?"

"The letters changed everything."

"Why?" she asked pulling her knees up to her chest and hugging them.

"Because, for the first time, I realized that you never really left me. Physically you were gone, but in your heart you never gave up. That means everything to me, Jenna. Everything."

"What are you saying, Kyle?" she asked softly. He could tell she was scared that he was going to yank the rug from under her yet again.

Instead of saying the words, he scooted closer and pulled her into his lap. She let out a gasp, but his mouth was covering hers so quickly that she didn't have time to speak. With one arm wrapped around her waist, he dug his fingers into her hair and pulled her closer, deepening his warm kiss. She reached around his neck and pulled him as close as she could get him, aching for more of his touch.

Pulling back, she looked into his eyes as she stroked the side of his jaw. "Kyle, what does this mean?" she whispered with a hint of fear in her voice.

"It means that I never want to be without you again. Do you understand me, Jenna Davis? My heart can't take it. If we move forward like this, you have to promise me that it's for forever."

"I promise, Kyle. Forever," she said softly as she leaned in to kiss him again.

JENNA COULDN'T BELIEVE this was finally happening. At first, she'd wanted to kill Becca for divulging her secret, but that quickly faded as Kyle spoke the words she'd been longing to hear since the day she left him.

Everything she'd ever wanted had always been just around the corner in January Cove, but to her it had always seemed a million miles away. Nick had damaged her self confidence so much that she'd never ventured even a small hope that one day she'd be back in January Cove with the true love of her life.

"You awake?" he asked as he stroked her temple with his finger. The sun was just starting to peek through the closed window blinds. They'd spent the night talking - and kissing -and eventually fell asleep in each other's arms.

"Yeah, I'm awake," she said, still unable to wipe the silly smile off her face.

"I need to tell you something," he said softly as his hand caressed her cheek.

"What?"

"I'm sorry."

"Kyle, you have nothing to be sorry for. This whole thing, all these years apart, was my fault."

"Not totally."

"What are you talking about?"

"I should have fought for you, Jenna. I should have confronted Nick sooner and brought you home. I should have known that you were waiting for me... "

"I wasn't waiting for you to rescue me, Kyle. That wasn't your responsibility."

"I was just so heartbroken, and I didn't think you'd come home with me."

"Let's put it behind us now, okay?" she said sitting up on her elbow and looking into his eyes. "From now on, we're together. No more running." Kyle smiled down at her and kissed her on the nose.

"And we're going to handle Nick together from now on. I have an attorney friend that will make sure things are settled so that Kaitlyn can have a good life no matter what. Okay?"

"I believe you, Kyle. I know you would do anything for Kaitlyn."

"I would, Jenna. I already love her." Jenna's eyes filled with tears. "Whether Nick is around or not won't really matter because I'm going to shower Kaitlyn with a real father's love, no matter what that man does."

"Thank you," she whispered softly as she laid her head on his chest.

"A new beginning," he said as he hugged her close.

"A new beginning," she repeated as she snuggled in and held onto him with everything she had.

GET a list of all of Rachel Hanna's books at www. RachelHannaAuthor.com.